THE HOPE IN HOT CHOCOLATE

a *Poppy Creek* novel

RACHAEL BLOOME

Cover design: Ana Grigoriu-Voicu with Books-design

Editing: Krista Dapkey with KD Proofreading

Proofing: Beth Attwood

SERIES READING ORDER

The Clause in Christmas

The Truth in Tiramisu

The Secret in Sandcastles

The Meaning in Mistletoe

The Faith in Flowers

The Whisper in Wind

The Hope in Hot Chocolate

Violet,

I love you more than words

LETTER FROM THE AUTHOR

Dear friend,

Hope is a theme that is close to my heart. In fact, it's present in all my books in some form or another. In this story, I explore the kind of hope found in unwavering, sacrificial love. But I'd be remiss if I didn't mention a greater hope—the ultimate hope—found in our Heavenly Father. In Him, we have assurance for today and for eternity. It's a precious gift that can't be stolen and is available to all (John 3:16-17).

As you read Sadie and Landon's story, may you be encouraged. Sometimes the darkness in the world can feel far too formidable, but love can make even the bleakest moments a whole lot brighter.

I'd love to chat more! You can reach me via email at hello@rachaelbloome.com, through my website, or in my private Facebook group, Rachael Bloome's Secret Garden Book Club.

. . .

Until next time,
Happy Reading!

Rachael Bloome

CHAPTER 1

The collage of ominous red numbers cluttering the spreadsheet glared accusingly, stating the obvious.

She was in trouble.

Without shifting her gaze from the laptop screen, Sadie Hamilton reached for another hazelnut truffle and popped it into her mouth.

Big trouble.

Of course, she'd been in tough situations before.

Like the time she forgot to place an entire custom order of caramel amaretto bonbons into the cooler before closing the sweet shop… on the hottest day in August. The next morning, she'd arrived to find fifty painstakingly handcrafted chocolates melted into unattractive lumps of goo. Luckily, the customer had been more than happy to substitute his order with the rarer, and much more expensive, almond and apricot liqueur bonbons she made only once a year from locally sourced apricots.

But this time?

She didn't know how she'd get herself out of this mess.

Her anxiety mounting, she polished off another truffle, but the momentary calm provided by the creamy chocolate and crunch of buttery hazelnuts didn't last long.

The sweet shop had never been in this much debt before, thanks to the unexpected repairs and new equipment she'd needed to purchase. Even with Valentine's Day around the corner, and the inevitable uptick in sales, she wasn't sure how much longer she'd survive.

She grasped for another truffle, but her fingertips met the cool porcelain plate instead.

How many chocolates had she brought into her office that morning? She couldn't remember. But she'd devoured every single one, as had become her habit on Monday mornings when she went over the previous week's numbers.

Maybe gobbling up the merchandise wasn't such a great idea.

Not that selling a few extra truffles would save her now.

Sadie glanced over her shoulder at the photograph hanging on the back wall, the special day it captured still vivid in her mind.

Her grandmother, the indelible Brigitte "Gigi" Durand, grinned at her from behind the thin layer of dust coating the glass. The tiny crumb of a woman barely reached five foot two inches, even in her flashy patent-leather boots, but she commanded a room—make that a *continent*—as if she were over ten feet tall. And it wasn't only because of her dramatic red hair dye that reminded Sadie of the chili peppers they used in their firecracker bonbons. Or her vibrant and colorful wardrobe of vintage pieces that never matched yet somehow looked chic and fashion-forward.

While both characteristics certainly made her stand out, it was Gigi's vivacious, fearless personality that won the hearts of everyone she met. Even in her eighties, she could conquer any challenge with grace, style, and genuine benevolence, and she didn't need a man to hold her hand while doing it.

As Rosie the Riveter inspired millions of working women, even after World War II, Gigi Durand was the cover model for strong, single females.

At least, she was to Sadie.

Ever since her parents passed away when she was nine, and Gigi stepped in to raise her, she'd idolized the older woman. More than that, she owed her everything.

How could she live with herself if she let Gigi down?

As she gazed at the photograph, tears of defeat and discouragement stung the backs of her eyes, blurring their smiling faces and creating a stark contrast to the happiness of that day.

They'd just won an award for Best Local Business, which not only included their small yet quaint hometown of Poppy Creek but all the neighboring provinces clustered in the idyllic foothills of Northern California.

In the slightly yellowed snapshot, they proudly brandished the gold-embossed certificate as they posed in front of their sweet shop. The sweet shop Gigi had named after Sadie and handed down to her, trusting her implicitly. The sweet shop that was now on the verge of failure after nearly three decades of unwavering success.

Rubbing her damp, itchy eyes, she returned her attention to the glowing laptop screen.

The numbers hadn't changed.

Although admittedly irrational, a small part of her had hoped she'd been imagining them, that she'd turn back around, and everything would have sorted itself out.

But life didn't work like that, did it?

The bell above the front door chimed, signaling that Tracey Peters, the fresh-out-of-high-school apprentice she'd hired part-time, had arrived for her morning shift. The girl's bright, youthful optimism was exactly what she needed to overcome her melancholy mood.

Within seconds of entering the main room of the sweet shop, the comforting aroma of rich chocolate and tantalizing vanilla bean lifted some of the tension from her neck and shoulders. Ever since she was a little girl, this place had been her haven, with its polished cherrywood countertops and glittering glass cases filled with tempting truffles and bonbons and old-fashioned taffy and caramels. They even had more unconventional offerings, like crystallized sugar crafted to resemble colorful quartz and geodes, which were especially popular among tourists and their children thanks to the town's historic mining roots.

Every single customer who walked through the front door left with a smile on their face, something sweet to savor, and a sense of joy and contentment they hadn't possessed when they'd entered.

How could she let this place close?

"Morning, boss!" Tracey chirped, looping an apron over her messy bun of cotton candy–colored hair.

"Good morning." Sadie smiled, taking in the girl's unusual—though surprisingly flattering—hairstyle choice.

It seemed like every week Tracey showed up with a new shade. Lemon-drop yellow. Licorice red. Even candy cane stripes at Christmastime.

Sadie ran a hand over her own caramel-colored strands, subconsciously smoothing back the flyaways.

Between Tracey's kaleidoscope of hues and Gigi's flamboyant ensembles, Sadie's everyday attire of jeans, a simple sweater, and an ever-so-practical ponytail looked downright drab in comparison. Not that she had the time or inclination for anything more adventurous.

"Want me to start by arranging the bonbons in the display cases this morning?" Tracey asked, slipping on a pair of protective gloves.

"That would be great. And I experimented with a new recipe yesterday. I'd love your opinion." While the almond butter and chocolate ganache had a pleasant enough flavor, they were missing the wow factor she'd been hoping for. A pinprick of self-doubt pierced her heart. Had she lost her touch?

"You know me, always happy to lend my taste buds," Tracey said with a laugh.

As she headed toward the kitchen, which also housed the coolers that kept the chocolates chilled overnight, a loud *thwack* thudded against the wall, startling them both.

"Not again," Sadie groaned.

"When are they going to be done?" Tracey asked with equal exasperation.

Sadie gritted her teeth as more hammering and pounding shook the wall separating their shop from the one next door, rattling the antique jars filled with an assortment of sweet and sour suckers.

The new owner had assured her that they'd barely notice the construction. Ha! She should've known better than to trust someone who didn't like candy, even if he had the kind of magnetic charm and good looks that could melt a bar of chocolate.

Not that they would work on her.

While Sadie tried to be patient, the constant chaos and commotion needed to stop. And not just for her own sanity. It disturbed the cozy and peaceful atmosphere she worked hard to cultivate for her customers.

How could someone select the perfect, buttery peanut brittle or smooth, delicate swirl of caramel and pralines when they feared any moment the roof might collapse on their head?

The clamor of breaking glass yanked Sadie from her agitated thoughts.

"What was that?" She frantically scanned the shelf of vintage candy dishes, some of which Gigi had brought back from her world travels and were irreplaceable.

"It sounded like it came from your office." Tracey stared wide-eyed at the open doorway, as though afraid of what they might find on the other side.

Her pulse matching the riotous rhythm of the unrelenting hammer and drill, Sadie hastened to assess the damage. A dismayed gasp escaped her lips when she spotted the framed photograph lying facedown on the aged hardwood floor.

Crouching beside it, she tentatively tipped it upright.

A long, jagged crack spliced through the unsuspecting smile of her younger self as she stood beside Gigi holding one edge of their Best Local Business award.

Even worse—the one-of-a-kind, hand-carved frame Gigi purchased in Indonesia had splintered up the side.

Was it an omen?

Don't be ridiculous, she scolded herself, shifting the blame to the one person who'd become the bane of her existence, business rival, and all-around nuisance ever since he moved into town a few months ago.

And it was time to give him a piece of her mind.

~

Landon Morris leaned in, trying to hear the foreman over the cacophony of power tools.

At six foot one, he had at least five inches on the guy, but what the foreman lacked in height and build, he more than made up for with skill and proficiency. While his crew didn't come cheap, they were the best, and Landon wouldn't settle for anything less.

Especially not on this project.

So far, the renovations were on track to meet his deadline.

Until today.

"Back order?" Landon groaned. "For how long?"

"Six weeks, at least," the foreman shouted over the offbeat percussion of dueling hammers. "There was some mix-up with the manufacturer."

No, no, no....

Landon suppressed his growing frustration, knowing it wasn't the foreman's fault. Things happened. But six weeks was unacceptable. He needed to open his doors to the public before that.

"There's a knockoff brand we could get right away, but they don't meet all your requirements."

Landon wasn't surprised. It wasn't easy to find ethically and sustainably sourced building materials, and they'd spent weeks locating the right company. There was no second choice. "Give me the phone number of the guy you've been talking to, and I'll see what I can work out."

He didn't add the last part of his thought: *because money talks.*

As a general rule, he didn't like flaunting his wealth and influence, but there were a few occasions when he needed to play the billionaire card.

This was one of those times.

Landon swept his gaze around the current war zone that encompassed his latest pet project. He'd known it would take a lot of work to transform the ancient and outdated shoe repair shop into the sleek, innovative space he'd imagined, but he'd assumed it would be fairly straightforward—nothing he couldn't handle. After all, before the age of thirty, he'd turned a single product—a biodegradable straw that didn't turn soggy in a glass of soda—into a billion-dollar sustainable packaging company based in Silicon Valley. Not to mention the countless nonprofits he ran on the side.

How hard could it be to open one measly shop in a sleepy little blip on the map like Poppy Creek?

Apparently, harder than he thought.

Especially if he wanted to meet his goal of opening before all the tourists converged in town for the Sips & Sweets Festival at the end of February.

This close to the wire, setbacks weren't an option.

Neither were distractions.

As if on cue, the walking distraction herself barged through the front door, her sharp, hazel eyes locking on to him like a riflescope.

From the first moment he met Sadie Hamilton at his friend Grant's wedding last year, she'd gotten under his skin with her bewitching blend of feisty, take-no-nonsense moxie and innate sweetness that lent a surprising—and irritatingly irresistible—softness to her blunt edges.

She reminded him of why he fell in love with chemistry at a young age—you could take two opposing compounds that shouldn't go together and create something even more spectacular than the sum of its parts.

The only problem?

Her life's work represented everything he stood against.

There wasn't a single profession he loathed more than sugar peddlers. As far as he was concerned, they were just as bad as tobacco companies. Maybe even worse, since cigarettes came with warning labels while sugar not only boldly touted a nostalgic innocence, it lurked in unusual places like whole wheat pasta and organic tomato sauce, tricking unsuspecting shoppers into consuming dangerous amounts.

A fact that hit too close to home.

"Excuse me? Did you hear what I said?"

Shoot. She'd been talking, and he hadn't heard a word. "Sorry, it's a little loud in here." He offered the feeble excuse, determined to pay closer attention. She may be Enemy Number One, but he still wanted to be a good neighbor.

"That's my point," Sadie repeated. "It's *too* loud. And all the hammering and drilling is rattling the wall between our shops." She brandished a photograph with a crack in the glass and a damaged frame. "See? This fell a few minutes ago."

He winced, genuinely remorseful. "Sorry about that. I'll get it fixed." He plucked the frame from her hand, their fingers grazing in the process. Ignoring the unexpected twinge of electricity, he added, "And I'll ask the guys to be more careful."

She blinked, as though she hadn't expected him to be so cooperative. "Thank you. And quieter? I understand you have work to do, but the constant noise is adversely affecting the ambiance of my shop. When people buy candy, they want to be happy and relaxed, not stressed and on edge."

His cynical expression must have given him away because both of her eyebrows arched.

"Is there something you'd like to say?" An icy chill crept into her tone, matching the frigid, wintery air outside.

Leave it alone, man. Don't poke the bear.

Unfortunately, he ignored his own sage advice. "Just that I'd find it hard to relax knowing sugar can spike insulin and lead to an unpleasant crash a few hours after consumption. But I can ask the crew to keep it down as much as possible without impeding their work."

Her cheeks reddened at his remark, although, to her credit, she kept her cool. "Thank you."

Without so much as a goodbye, she spun on her heel. But halfway to the door, she swirled around, meeting his gaze. "Just so you know, chocolate is scientifically proven to produce dopamine, serotonin, and endorphins, all of which are mood boosters. Some studies show that even *thinking* about eating a piece of chocolate can increase the body's production of pleasure chemicals." Not waiting for a response, she slipped outside.

Landon watched her quick strides through the large picture window, admittedly impressed.

She could hold her own—a trait he admired.

Although, he couldn't help thinking that if she knew what he did, she might change her position.

For now, they'd have to agree to disagree.

And considering the jumble of conflicting emotions she elicited each time she came around, he'd be better off keeping his distance.

At least, as much as he could avoid someone who worked next door.

CHAPTER 2

That evening, Sadie flipped the wooden sign to Closed on the shop's front door before stepping into the frosty night air. A biting breeze nipped at her neck, and she flipped up the collar of her red peacoat, smiling at the festive storefronts facing the town square.

She adored Poppy Creek this time of year. The historic gold rush town came alive as a living, breathing Valentine's Day card, with the stone, brick, and shiplap buildings draped in red and pink garlands and twinkling lights, and the frosted window panes hand-painted with decorative hearts and flowers. She didn't even mind the cold, blustery weather.

Sure, there were times she daydreamed about traveling the world like Gigi, exploring exciting, glamorous locales like New York and Paris, but she knew she wouldn't be able to stay away from her hometown for long. Not only did running the sweet shop encompass her entire life, the townspeople had become her surrogate family.

Up ahead, two of her best friends, Cassie Davis and Eliza Parker, who co-owned The Calendar Café, closed up shop and headed toward the town hall, a large, one-room building constructed in the late 1800s that worked overtime as a meeting center, local theater, and art and dance studio.

Tonight, Mayor Burns planned to announce the final details of the highly anticipated Sips & Sweets Festival.

Every year, bakers, chocolatiers, winemakers, and other artisans from the surrounding areas gathered in the town square on one magical evening, offering a smorgasbord of the most mouthwatering delights imaginable. In addition to the caloric cornucopia, festivalgoers enjoyed live music, raffles, and the crème de la crème—the Tastiest Treat competition, when culinary craftsmen unveiled their unique and tantalizing creations, vying for the honor of first place.

This year, Sadie was even more determined to win the grand prize. Not only would she benefit from the exposure of the featured article in *Sweet Destinations,* a nationally recognized magazine, the five-thousand-dollar prize would go a long way toward paying down her debts.

She just had one problem.

The judges wanted something new and inventive along with an unforgettable flavor experience.

And so far, she didn't have a single good idea.

Tucking her self-doubt into the back of her mind, she opened the creaking wooden door and welcomed the rush of warmth that enveloped her. The potbelly stove in the corner, along with the plethora of townspeople packed inside, rendered her heavy coat unnecessary. She draped it over her arm, searching the sea of smiling faces for one in particular.

She noticed Dolores Whittaker near the refreshment table, chatting with the town librarian, Beverly Barrie. Though both women were Gigi's age, they couldn't be more different. Beverly, with her graceful frame and silvery hair swept into a simple chignon, embodied timeless elegance à la Grace Kelly, while Dolores's plump physique, pile of cropped white curls, and Coke-bottle glasses reminded Sadie of a grandmotherly Mrs. Claus.

While she loved both women dearly, she needed to get Dolores alone.

Catching her eye, she waved hello and nodded toward the back of the room.

Dolores politely excused herself and shuffled over to meet her, her blue eyes shimmering expectantly. "You remembered?"

"How could I forget?" Sadie dug inside her purse and retrieved a small square box tied with a red satin ribbon with gold filigree. She handed it to Dolores with a smile.

The older woman cradled it against her chest like a precious family heirloom, her gaze distant and glassy, as though she'd momentarily been transported to a happier time.

This is what Sadie loved most about her job.

She didn't just give people a fleeting, flavorful treat. Beloved sweets, like chocolate, had the power to evoke memories and real, tangible feelings associated with a specific time and place.

And more importantly, a specific person.

Today was Dolores's anniversary, and every year to celebrate, her husband, Arthur, ordered the same box of chocolates—cherry cordials. First from Gigi, then from Sadie when she took over the shop.

And each year since he'd passed away, Sadie continued the tradition on his behalf.

"You don't have to keep doing this, dear," Dolores murmured with a warble in her voice.

"Of course I do," Sadie said with warm conviction. "Arthur

had a standing order at the shop. And as long as I'm standing, I'll see that it's delivered."

Dolores met her gaze, her grateful tears magnified behind the thick lenses. "Thank you," she whispered, still clutching the chocolates to her heart.

Sadie leaned in for a gentle hug and whispered, "Happy Anniversary, DeeDee."

Feeling a slight catch in her throat, Sadie pulled away, thankful when Mayor Burns called the meeting to order from the front of the room before she lost her composure.

With her prized treasure tucked beneath her arm, Dolores rejoined Beverly, and Sadie searched for Cassie and Eliza, spotting them in the back row.

Both women waved, motioning that they'd saved her a seat.

"Aren't you excited?" Eliza gushed under her breath, her huge, dark eyes bright and sparkling. "I heard there are double the contestants this year."

Sadie swallowed, her mouth suddenly dry. Double the entries? That didn't bode well for her chances of winning, especially considering her recent lack of inspiration.

Of course, Sadie doubted Eliza was worried about the extra competition. The petite blonde baker extraordinaire had a flair for concocting the most unexpected yet delicious desserts on the planet, starting with her famed tiramisu cheesecake.

"Do you know what you're entering?" Sadie whispered, trying to still the nervous flutter in her stomach.

"I have a few ideas." Eliza flashed a mischievous smirk.

"And she won't give me any hints," Cassie said with a playful pout, adding, "For fun, we're keeping our entries a secret until the festival, which is easier said than done. Luke has become my primary taste tester, and he's been bouncing off the walls from all the caffeine." She laughed softly, her green eyes taking on an affectionate glow when she mentioned her husband.

Although a relative newcomer to town, Cassie had an excellent shot at winning the competition, too. The woman was a veritable magician with an espresso wand, conjuring up elaborate and ingenious lattes that both surprised and pleased the palate.

"What about you?" Cassie asked.

Sadie shifted on the wooden folding chair, too embarrassed to confess her creative slump. "Not yet, but I'm working on it."

"Whatever you come up with will be fabulous," Cassie offered kindly. "Luke brought home a box of your marshmallow mint chocolates the other day and I can't stop eating them."

Sadie smiled her thanks, grateful for the vote of confidence.

With renewed determination, she resolved to hire Tracey for a couple of extra shifts and lock herself in the kitchen without distractions for the next few days.

Feeling bolstered by her plan, she focused her attention on Mayor Burns, who opened the meeting with another one of his long-winded introductions.

Truthfully, the man had never been her favorite person. He always seemed a little too showy. Too slick. Like he cared more about the position of power than the townspeople. A fact that had never been clearer to Sadie than when he approved Landon's proposal to open a rival business next door to hers.

Although Landon wanted to keep the exact nature of his

new shop under wraps until the grand opening, he'd let one detail slip, and it had already made its rounds through the rumor mill. According to her sources, he planned on selling "something to satisfy your sweet tooth without all the sugar."

While it sounded like nonsense, Sadie couldn't rule out the threat he posed to her already struggling business. He had billions of dollars to back whatever ridiculous idea he'd concocted. Plus, it was common knowledge the man had a personal vendetta against sweets. Over a year ago, he'd gone on record in several interviews stating that sugar was an addiction destroying America.

She strongly suspected that if she had to shutter her doors for good, he'd be on the sidewalk applauding.

The thought made her shiver, along with the door opening, letting in a gust of frosty air.

As she glanced over her shoulder, her heart froze.

Landon hovered by the doorway, noticing a flicker of annoyance distort Mayor Burns's features at the intrusion. But as quickly as everyone glanced over their shoulders to assess the latecomer, they redirected their focus to the front of the room.

Everyone, that is, except for Sadie.

From the corner of his eye, he detected a faint glimmer of confusion and disapproval in her glower, as if she expected his arrival to be a mistake and hoped he'd turn around and march back outside any second.

He'd have to disappoint her yet again.

Ever since he moved to town, she'd seemed to take his

presence as a personal offense, like he existed to make her life more difficult.

Of course, the truth was far more complicated.

Both regarding his reasons for moving to Poppy Creek and the emotional tug of war he experienced around Sadie Hamilton and her sweet shop.

Lost in his thoughts, Landon leaned against the back wall, barely paying attention to Burns's never-ending monologue. He perked up when he heard the man say, "Now, for the last item on tonight's agenda."

Burns rifled through some papers on the podium as if biding his time before announcing, "To accommodate the unexpected increase in entrants for the Tastiest Treat competition this year, a few of you will need to share a booth at the festival. We will still judge your entries separately, but we do ask that you make the look and theme of your booth cohesive. You'll find the names of those being asked to share on the bulletin board in back. All pairings are final. I appreciate your cooperation."

Landon suppressed a snort, knowing that was code for *Suck it up and don't complain.*

Out of curiosity, he wandered over to the corkboard as Burns wrapped up the meeting and townspeople shuffled out of their seats.

What poor souls would have to share their coveted space? He had big plans for his booth and had zero interest in compromising his vision to accommodate a partner. Of course, he and Burns had an understanding. He wouldn't find his name on the list.

As he scanned the lineup of unlucky entrants, his pulse skidded to a halt.

No, that can't be right....

He stared at the two names printed side by side, focusing all his energy on the letters as if he could rearrange them into a different configuration by sheer willpower.

There had to be some mistake. He couldn't share a booth with Sadie Hamilton. Not in a million years. It would be like mixing nitric acid and hydrazine—unstable and explosive.

He'd have a talk with Mayor Burns and sort something out. If he acted quickly, maybe he could fix the situation before Sadie saw—

A loud sigh echoed behind him.

He turned to see a frown on Sadie's face that matched his sentiments exactly.

Although, for some reason, he felt a faint stab of disappointment at her obvious displeasure.

She recovered quickly, forcing a tight smile. "Looks like we got the short straw."

"Yeah, it's not ideal. I'm firmly set on my plans for my booth. If it's okay with you, I thought I'd talk to Burns about—"

Landon paused when Mayor Burns rapped his gavel against the wooden podium in response to some collective grumbling. "Look, everyone. I realize the change in plans will require some of you to be flexible. But try to make the best of it. As I said, all pairings are final."

Excited chatter drew Landon's attention to Cassie and Eliza, who seemed elated to be teamed up. They immediately bent their heads together, already strategizing their joint effort.

Landon observed Sadie watching them with a wistful expression.

Once again, he experienced a tiny tug on his heart that he couldn't explain.

He cleared his throat, mentally repeating Burns's directive to make the best of the situation. "Well, that's that. I guess we should get together sometime soon and decide how we want to tackle this."

"Uh-huh," she murmured, slowly coming to grips with the reality of the situation. Then, as if a realization had dawned on her, she brightened. "I suppose if we're sharing a booth, you'll have to tell me what kind of business you're opening."

Shoot. He hadn't considered that. "I suppose so," he said noncommittally.

"Why don't we meet up tomorrow evening after I close the shop?"

He couldn't help noting her sudden burst of enthusiasm. "That works. Can you be at my place by six o'clock?" If he was going to let her in on his secret project, he wanted to do it on his own terms.

A flash of hesitation sparked in her eyes, but she shrugged. "Sure. I can do that."

"Great. I'll see you then," he said by way of goodbye.

Halfway to the door, he pulled his cell phone out of his coat pocket to make the necessary arrangements for tomorrow night.

It would be late notice, but he'd make it work.

He could only hope his last-minute plan didn't backfire.

CHAPTER 3

As soon as the stately stone mansion came into view, Landon relaxed his grip on the steering wheel, the welcoming sight stirring a smile.

The moment he'd made the impulsive decision to uproot his life—and his mother's—and move them to the middle of nowhere, he'd assumed he'd have to build a custom home. Then he saw a dream listing. The real estate agent called it an "elegant escape to the English countryside nestled in the comforting oasis of Poppy Creek." It had been built in the late 1800s by an eccentric couple who'd struck it rich during the gold rush, making the unique structure a well-known landmark in the area.

While he'd done extensive remodeling, including retrofitting the entire place to be wheelchair accessible, the bones of the home were perfect. He loved everything about it, from the stunning English architecture to the ivy-covered exterior to the scenic location on the edge of Willow Lake.

Even his hard-to-please mother had been impressed when she first laid eyes on it. Not that she'd admit it.

Irene Morris seemed allergic to finding pleasure or approval in anything these days. Although Landon wouldn't give up trying.

"Hey, Mom." He found her in her usual spot in the library and bent down to plant a kiss on her cheek before settling in the armchair opposite her, relishing the warmth of the crackling fire. "How was your day?"

"Fine." She glanced up from the worn pages of her classic novel and managed a slight smile. It didn't reach her dark eyes, but at least it softened some of the harsh lines that aged her far beyond her sixty-two years.

He hadn't seen his mother truly smile in years, and it pained him to witness her natural beauty and brilliance fade even deeper into the gloom of her depression.

"Have you been outside today?" He surreptitiously surveyed her wheelchair, searching for traces of dirt, leaves, or twigs in the tread.

"Do you mean outside the house or outside this room?"

"Either."

"Why would I do that when I have everything I need right here?" Her gaze swept the labyrinth of leather-bound books landing on the idyllic indoor garden behind them.

The library and conservatory combination had been the biggest selling point when he'd shown her the house, and he couldn't blame her. The haven of mahogany bookshelves and glass-and-wrought-iron greenhouse belonged in the pages of a fairy tale. Not to mention the intoxicating aroma of aged paper and fragrant foliage.

While he was pleased she loved the space, the whole purpose of moving to Poppy Creek had been to draw her out of her troubling isolation, not make it worse.

"What about human interaction and conversation?" he asked, tempering his disappointment.

As if responding to his question, a mound of dark brown fur snoozing in front of the fireplace raised its small, angular face to glare at him.

"Did you hear that, Reginald?" Irene asked the affronted dachshund. "Apparently, Landon doesn't consider you adequate company."

With his pointed chin lifted high in the air, Reginald slipped from his regal dog bed of plush purple velvet and gold tassels and waddled to her side.

"No offense, Reggie," Landon offered, though the pup didn't appear appeased as he sought comforting head scratches from his doting owner. "But, Mom, you must admit it would be nice to have a conversation with a human being every once in a while. Other than me and Gladys."

The kindhearted housekeeper had been a godsend, but Landon wanted his mother to make genuine friends and find a community, a support system. He'd seen Poppy Creek work its small-town magic on others—heck, it had even worked on him—why couldn't his mother give the town a chance?

"I get all the mental stimulation I need right here." She tapped the open book in her lap. "Now, enough about me. Tell me about your day."

He buried a sigh, agreeing to let the topic drop for now. "It was… eventful."

"Care to elaborate?" Irene prompted, scratching behind one of Reginald's oversized ears. The pup's bruised ego seemed adequately soothed.

"There's been a hiccup with the Tastiest Treat competition. I have to share my booth at the festival."

"Oh, dear." Irene frowned.

Landon had told her all about his over-the-top idea, and she knew how critical it was to make a good impression when he unveiled his new business venture. It was risky, to say the least, especially in a town famous for its nostalgic, old-fashioned charm. He needed everything to go smoothly.

"Surely when you explain to them how important the booth is to you, they'll go along with your idea."

"You don't know Sadie," Landon grunted. He had a feeling she'd love to see his business fail.

"Sadie, huh?" Irene mused. "Is she young?"

"A few years younger than me, maybe. Why?"

"Is she attractive?"

"Why does that matter?"

"No reason." Irene continued to stroke Reginald's head, but the glint in her eyes belied her feigned innocence.

"Don't get any ideas, Mom. Nothing is going to happen between me and Sadie. We don't exactly get along."

"And why not?"

"Let's just say we're very different people."

"Like Elizabeth Bennet and Mr. Darcy." She drummed her fingers on the book again.

"This isn't one of your novels. There is no underlying romantic tension or happily ever after on the horizon."

"If you say so." She didn't look convinced.

"Seriously, Mom. I'll be lucky if she doesn't try to sabotage my contest entry. Or at best, inadvertently ruin my chances of winning by being completely uncooperative."

"I see." She pondered his grim prediction a moment before adding, "Well, this experience might be good for you."

"How so?" he asked, although he wasn't keen to hear her answer. Nothing good could come from working alongside Sadie Hamilton. Of that, he was certain.

"It's no secret that you have an intense need to control everything, despite the fact that isn't how life works. It will be good for you to loosen the reins a little."

Landon bristled, thinking of all the turmoil, confusion, and utter helplessness that had comprised his life over the past year and a half. Didn't she understand what made him this way?

Instead of verbalizing a far too painful truth, he said, "You could be right." Summoning a smile, he rose. "I should get to bed since I have an early start tomorrow." With a tight ache in his chest, he planted another kiss on her cheek, adding, "Don't stay up too late."

As he mechanically went through the motions of his nightly routine, her words hovered over him, repeating like a haunting melody in his mind.

How could he loosen the reins when his unrelenting grip was the only thing keeping their family from falling apart?

~

As Sadie turned down the quiet, tree-lined lane and approached the buttery-cream farmhouse with toffee-colored trim, some of the tension from the tumultuous day left her taut shoulders.

She couldn't wait to see Gigi, who always knew how to lift her spirits.

Her smile widened when she parked beside Gigi's red Cadillac DeVille and spotted the glittering gold Mercedes on the other side, which meant she'd find her best friend, Lucy Gardener, inside, too.

Her tread lighter now, Sadie bounded up the creaking porch steps and quickly crossed the wide veranda.

The welcoming scents of velvety chocolate and sweet plum preserves greeted her, and she followed the comforting aroma to the spacious kitchen down the hall.

When Gigi renovated the house back in the eighties, she'd borrowed square footage from the adjacent rooms to expand the kitchen, giving her plenty of space to comfortably create her tantalizing confections at home since, according to Gigi, one never knew when inspiration would strike.

Or in Sadie's case, when it *wouldn't* strike.

She found her grandmother drizzling melted white chocolate across a tray of silky black bonbons at the expansive center island while Lucy perched on a swiveling barstool, her long, willowy legs crossed gracefully at the ankles.

"Finally! Reinforcements are here," Lucy gushed, forgoing a hello. "Gigi said she needed a taste tester, and she's been force-feeding me chocolate for the last hour and a half. I'm not sure my clothes will fit by the time I leave." She laughed, tilting her head so her long blond hair spilled down her back.

"As you can see," Gigi interjected, her pale-green eyes twinkling as Lucy tossed another tasty morsel into her mouth, "she's suffering immensely."

Grinning at their banter, Sadie slipped out of her coat and laid it on the antique dining table near a tray of cooling truffles. Whenever Gigi returned from her travels, she couldn't resist toying with new recipes, as if the bottled-up ideas spilled out of her. "I take it the doctors ruled out chocolate as one of your migraine triggers?" she asked Lucy, relief rippling through her.

"Yep! After months of keeping a tedious food journal, I'm finally in the clear," Lucy told her happily. "And I can still have cottage cheese, sauerkraut, and pickled okra."

"Thank goodness for that," Sadie teased, settling on the barstool beside her.

A few months ago, Lucy started experiencing mysterious migraines, which sometimes left her completely immobilized. When Sadie first learned of the episodes, she'd been a wreck, stressing about every worst-case scenario. Although, she'd tried to hide her fears, not wanting to add to her friend's list of worries.

Thankfully, the doctors had ruled out the serious, life-threatening causes and were now working their way through potential allergies and intolerances. While a part of her desperately wanted answers for her friend, she'd readily admit her delight that chocolate wasn't the culprit.

"What are you sampling?" Sadie leaned across the counter, inhaling the sultry scent she couldn't quite place.

Gigi sprinkled a pinch of candied lemon peel over one of the bonbons before passing it to her. "Dark chocolate and a plum wine–preserve filling, topped with creamy white chocolate infused with a hint of orange blossom honey, followed by a lemon garnish."

"You'll want to eat the whole thing at once," Lucy advised. "Unless you don't mind the gooey center winding up on your clothes." She gestured to a purple stain on her designer sweater. "Totally worth it, though." She winked at Gigi.

Sadie popped the smooth sphere into her mouth as instructed, closing her eyes as it melted, releasing a symphony of flavors that all blended beautifully, one complementing the other, not competing in the slightest.

Although she'd been experimenting with unexpected combinations herself, all her recent efforts suddenly paled in comparison.

What had happened to her? Gigi had taught her everything

she'd learned under the tutelage of a renowned chocolatier in Paris, even claiming that Sadie had surpassed her own skills. But lately, nothing she made sparked the same fire in her bones. Nothing moved her. Had she completely lost her passion and creativity?

Her melancholy thoughts must have shown on her face because Gigi asked, "Is it that bad?"

Sadie swallowed and opened her eyes. "Not at all! It's amazing. Honestly. One of your best bonbons yet."

"Then why the long face, ma chérie?"

Sadie shifted on the barstool. If she confessed her troubles, Gigi would swoop in to rescue her, as she had her entire life. But her grandmother had already made enough sacrifices on her behalf. No, she needed to stand on her own two feet, no matter how shaking her footing became. "Sorry. It's been… a difficult day."

"What happened?" Lucy asked, while Gigi immediately set an antique copper pot on the stove. The same one she used every time she made her emergency hot chocolate that Sadie lovingly referred to as liquid comfort.

With a heavy sigh, she divulged the details of that morning's altercation with Landon, then explained how they'd been assigned to share a booth at the festival, leaving out the part about her utter lack of inspiration in the kitchen and lack of funds in the bank.

"Maybe it won't be as bad as you think," Lucy offered, ever the optimist.

"Thanks, but this is Landon Morris we're talking about." She gratefully accepted the mug Gigi slid across the counter and wrapped her hands around the smooth ceramic curves, soaking up the warmth. The familiar notes of chocolate and vanilla curled from the rim, instantly working their magic.

"I know he has some questionable opinions about a few things, but he isn't that bad," Lucy insisted. "In fact, Vick really likes him. We think you two might get along better than you think. Maybe you should give him a chance."

Sadie suppressed a retort by taking a sip of her drink, letting the rich, creamy beverage coat the back of her throat instead. Why was it that as soon as people found themselves in a relationship, they felt the need to pair up everyone around them? She loved her friend dearly, but her constant hints that she and Landon would make a good couple were beyond delusional, almost to the point of being insulting.

"I know you like to look for the best in people, Luce. But sometimes, what you see is what you get."

Despite Landon's superficial charms and undeniable good looks, she found nothing about the man appealing.

And no amount of cajoling by her matchmaking friends would change her mind.

CHAPTER 4

After another day of unsuccessfully creating an entry to impress the festival judges, the last thing Sadie wanted was to spend the evening with Landon Morris. But she also knew this was her chance to finally discover his plans for the shop next door. And her best shot at devising a strategy to fight the competition rested in knowing exactly what she was up against.

Her stomach clenched with nervous jitters as she parked in front of the sprawling mansion, suddenly feeling woefully underdressed in her jeans, scuffed ankle boots, and plain black sweater. The red peacoat Gigi bought her in Paris was the only thing that kept her from being embarrassingly blasé.

She quickly ran her fingers through her pin-straight hair in an attempt to add volume, then huffed in frustration. Why did she care how she looked? Landon's opinion of her appearance didn't matter in the slightest.

With an agitated jerk of her hands, she snapped her hair into its usual ponytail before slipping out of the vintage 1941 Ford panel truck Gigi had painted cherry red with Sadie's

Sweet Shop hand-lettered on the side in swirling gold calligraphy. It felt a little like parking an armored tank behind enemy lines.

As she climbed the stone steps, she paused at the sight of a wide ramp leading from the driveway to the imposing double doors. Had the ramp always been there or was it something Landon added?

Her curiosity piqued, she pressed the doorbell. An elegant chime echoed inside, followed by the faint clip-clop of chunky heels.

An older woman in her sixties or seventies flung open the door with a wide smile. "Good evening, dear! You must be Sadie." She maneuvered her broad, pleasantly round frame out of the doorway, waving her hand. "Come in, come in. You'll catch your death out here."

"Thank you." Sadie smiled, immediately charmed by the woman's friendly demeanor.

"I'm Gladys," she said, closing the door to the frosty night air. "I take care of the house for Mr. Landon."

Sadie suppressed a chuckle at her humorous mix of the formal title paired with his first name. Not to mention referring to the opulent estate as merely a *house*.

"That's quite a big job." Sadie admired the enormous entryway, glittering chandelier, and imperial staircase so expertly polished it gleamed.

"That it is, dear. But it's one I love. I've been a housekeeper my entire life, even for the occasional celebrity," she said with a twinkle in her eyes. "But Mr. Landon is by far my favorite employer."

Sadie found that hard to believe and wondered if he'd bugged the house so his staff was always on their best behavior, but she detected no guile in the woman's warm, weathered features.

"Follow me, dear. You can wait in the den while Mr. Landon wraps up a few final details with the pilot."

"Pilot?" Sadie repeated, startled.

"Yes, dear. Mr. Landon isn't rated to fly the jet by himself," she said as though it were the most casual sentence in the world.

"Jet?" Sadie echoed, embarrassed by her sudden inability to do anything except parrot the woman, but she was too stunned to say anything else.

Landon hadn't mentioned anything about *flying* anywhere. What exactly had she gotten herself into?

Although she didn't consider herself a materialistic person, or particularly swayed by the finer things, Sadie couldn't help being a tiny bit impressed by the private runway and jet, the posh car service that picked them up at the airport in San Francisco, and the secluded table at the Michelin-star restaurant.

She smoothed the silky soft, black bamboo napkin across her lap, grateful to partially hide her faded jeans. If she'd felt underdressed arriving at Landon's home, she now felt downright dowdy surrounded by couples dripping in designer duds and diamonds. She half expected Landon to be embarrassed by her, but his expression said the opposite.

He gazed at her across the table with a look that made heat travel up her neck. She had to admit, the man had the sexy smolder down to a science. But this wasn't a date. And she wouldn't be dazzled by an attractive smile, even if her traitorous hormones disagreed.

Averting her gaze, she guzzled her ice water.

"Is it too warm in here? I can ask them to turn down the heat."

"No, that's okay. I'm fine." She set down her glass, returning her hands to her lap where they could fidget with the napkin that probably cost more than her entire outfit.

Besides the fact that she'd never dream of changing the climate of an entire restaurant for her own comfort, she didn't want to admit that he affected her, let alone made her skin sizzle.

"So, what do you think of the place?" He gestured around the dimly lit room, and Sadie took in the luxurious decor that blended old-world opulence with sleek, minimalist design.

"It's lovely, but I still don't understand why we're here." The entire trip, he'd been secretive and tight-lipped, like someone planning a surprise party. It didn't make sense. "Aren't we supposed to be discussing our plans for the booth?"

"We will." He gifted her with a mischievous grin that resulted in another infuriating hot flash.

What was wrong with her? The guy wanted to put her out of business, for crying out loud. Rule number one for basic survival: Don't swoon over the enemy.

She downed another gulp of water as a server approached their table with their first course. At least, she assumed that's what it was. The food placed in front of them was unlike anything she'd ever seen before, as though it came from another planet.

She waited for the server to leave before asking, "What is it?"

A billowing mound of foam emitted some kind of aromatic steam that smelled heavenly.

"Have you ever had molecular gastronomy cuisine?"

"Molecular what?" Sadie leaned back as the fragrant steam spread across the tabletop like a filmy fog floating on a still lake.

"Molecular gastronomy. It's a scientific approach to food preparation that results in an unexpected and artistic culinary experience, like making pasta translucent or transforming something liquid into a foam or vapor," Landon explained. "It takes fine dining to a whole new level."

Skeptical, Sadie frowned. "But does it actually taste good?"

"You tell me." He nudged the plate of foam toward her with another one of his stomach-swirling smiles.

"Uh-uh. You first." She nudged it back.

"If you insist." He dug his spoon into the light, airy concoction and plopped it into his mouth.

She watched as he closed his eyes, pure elation crossing his features, reminding her of the look on her customers' faces when they tried her chocolates for the first time.

"Mm... even better than I remember," he murmured.

Intrigued, she picked up her spoon. "You're not messing with me, are you?"

He chuckled, and the throaty rumble roused dormant butterflies she resolutely ignored.

Tentatively, she scooped a small dollop onto her spoon and slipped it past her lips. Savory seasonings burst across her tongue, taking her by surprise. Her eyes widened as the familiar yet unexpected flavor notes registered on her taste buds. "It tastes like lobster bisque!"

"That's because it *is* lobster bisque," Landon said with a laugh. "Just not like you've ever had it before."

Mesmerized by the otherworldly experience, Sadie forgot all about the booth at the festival and her dislike of her dinner companion, wholly transfixed by each new entrée as the server brought wave upon wave of culinary delights, ranging from translucent ravioli with an aerated cream sauce to fried goat cheese foam bathed in a sage-flavored smoke.

Even more astounding than the food, Landon came alive as he explained the science behind the different cooking techniques, his passion evident in the way he made even the most technical, granular details captivating. She knew from interviews she'd read online that he had a degree in biochemical engineering, but she had no idea that his scientific interests extended to the kitchen.

Whether or not she wanted to admit it, she found his fervor infectious. It even reminded her of her own passion for making chocolate. At least, the passion she used to have.

Was it possible they actually had something in common?

As the last dish was carried away, a tall, striking man with hair as black as old-fashioned licorice drops approached their table. He greeted them with a smile. "How is everything tasting this evening?"

"Kaito!" Landon rose and gave the man a side hug. "You've outdone yourself tonight."

"Then everything is to your liking?" He spoke impeccable English with a faint accent Sadie couldn't place.

"Oishī," Landon said, patting him on the shoulder.

"Your Japanese is getting better." Kaito grinned.

Sadie watched the exchange with interest, marveling at the mutual respect and regard both men displayed toward one another.

"And what did you think?" Kaito asked, turning toward her with the same warm smile.

"It was incredible. I've never had a meal quite like it," she told him with complete sincerity.

He beamed, pleased by her compliment.

"Kaito is the chef and owner." Landon gazed at his friend with pride. "Thanks to his culinary genius, the restaurant became an overnight success and is still one of the top restaurants in the city over a year later."

"Landon is being modest. I wouldn't even have a restaurant if he hadn't believed in me and invested in my vision. I owe everything to this man."

Landon shuffled his feet, appearing uncomfortable under Kaito's praise.

To her chagrin, she found his modesty both unexpected and appealing.

"Are you two ready for dessert?" Kaito asked, lightening the mood.

"Dessert?" Sadie cast a furtive glance at Landon, knowing how he felt about the D-word.

Up until this point, the evening had been perfect. *Too* perfect.

It was time for the other Gucci loafer to drop.

Along with a much-needed dose of reality.

Landon stole a glance at Sadie as he said, "Absolutely!" and enjoyed the look of shock that crossed her face. Teasing her further, he tossed her a wink.

She gaped at him, dumbfounded, as Kaito left their table, and a moment later, a server arrived with a sampler of desserts.

"Let's see...." Landon surveyed the vivid assortment,

pointing to the various confectionaries as he called out their names. "We have liquid popcorn with caramel froth, chocolate caviar, violet ice cream dusted with candied lemon frost and lavender snow, and orange and mango spheres sprinkled with rose crystals."

"I don't understand. Don't these go against your no-sugar policy?"

He shifted on the slick leather chair, a surge of nervous energy rippling through him.

It was time he revealed his top-secret plan for his shop, the project he'd been working on for months. He needed her to be on board, not make it harder for him to win over the community with his outlandish idea.

The weight of this moment—and everything that was riding on it—pressed down on him, making it impossible to speak. What if she didn't react the way he hoped? What if his intentions for the evening backfired?

"Landon?" she prompted, as if sensing he'd gotten lost in his thoughts.

He cleared his throat, convincing himself that his fears were unfounded. He'd seen the way she lit up with excitement as each new dish arrived at their table. She'd become enamored with the magic of it all, he could tell.

It was all going to be fine.

"You're right," he told her after gathering a deep breath. "I wouldn't normally indulge in dessert, but the thing that's so fascinating about molecular gastronomy is that it doesn't just change the appearance of the food, it changes the way the body metabolizes it, too. Some critics argue that the chemical transformation robs the food of some of its nutritional value, but what they don't acknowledge is that it can also reduce some of the negative qualities, too."

"You mean, like less sugar?"

"Exactly. Which means desserts like this are much healthier than what people traditionally consume after a meal." He paused, gauging her reaction, but her expression remained unreadable.

In too deep to turn back now, he forged ahead. "In a lot of ways, molecular gastronomy is like performing magic. And I'd like to bring that magic to Poppy Creek. Starting with my entry for the Tastiest Treat competition. I'm calling it a Strawberry Shortcake Cloud. It'll taste just like regular strawberry shortcake but with a fraction of the calories and sugar, and it'll float on your plate like... Well, like a cloud. The booth itself will have a Willy Wonka vibe, a blend of chemistry and confection. What do you think?"

He sucked in a breath, surprised by how desperately he wanted her to like the idea. At some point throughout the evening, his need for her approval had grown from purely business to personal.

"Let me get this straight," she said slowly. "You're opening a molecular gastronomy restaurant in Poppy Creek?"

"Not a restaurant, per se. More of an à la carte experience. Customers can order a scoop of ice cream or cup of hot chocolate, but it'll be served in a way they've never seen before. It'll—"

"Satisfy their sweet tooth without all the sugar," she murmured.

"Exactly." Landon leaned forward, so close to reaching her with his vision. Now, to drive the point home. "Sadie, I want to show people that they don't have to risk their health to satisfy their cravings. They can still indulge, but without the same level of negative consequences. They don't need—"

"Shops like mine," she interrupted quietly, staring at her hands folded in her lap.

"Well, no. I mean…" Landon hesitated, realizing he'd taken a wrong turn somewhere. "What I mean is—"

"I know exactly what you mean." She lifted her gaze, a mixture of sadness and outrage sparking in her hazel eyes. "You'd be more than happy to put places like mine out of business."

"That's not what I'm saying." A hardness settled in his stomach at the partial untruth.

Wasn't that exactly what he was saying? Sure, his biggest beef was with massive corporations who smuggled indecent amounts of sugar into everything from kids' cereal to supposed health foods, but didn't candy stores—even local mom-and-pop shops like Sadie's—contribute to the problem?

His head started to spin, and he struggled to regain control of his thoughts.

"I just—" He cleared his dry, scratchy throat. "I just want to change the culture around sugar consumption."

She straightened, raising her chin, her eyes flashing. "And by culture, you mean places where people go to buy candy and chocolates for their loved ones, be it to celebrate a special occasion or to offer comfort and condolences for a painful loss." Her voice trembled with righteous indignation, and she displayed a conscious effort to keep herself calm and under control. "Like it or not, Landon, sweets have been a part of our culture for centuries and they make people happy. What's so wrong with that?"

A response immediately bubbled to the surface, but he stopped himself just in time. It wasn't his story to tell. But what else could he say?

When the silence between them dragged on, Sadie crumpled her napkin on the table.

"I'd like to go home now, if that's okay."

Defeated, he nodded and said, "Of course," although it was the opposite of what he wanted.

He reached for his wallet, and in that moment, he had a sinking suspicion he'd lost a whole lot more than a disagreement.

CHAPTER 5

Sadie spent the entire trip home fuming in silence, wondering why she'd agreed to the evening in the first place.

She should have known something like this would happen. They clearly couldn't be in the same room together without clashing over their conflicting beliefs. How could they possibly share a booth at the festival? It would be a disaster.

Not to mention, he already had his entire display planned out to the smallest detail, making it painfully obvious he didn't intend to compromise.

Her stomach clenched. Because of Landon, she might lose her one opportunity to dig herself out of debt. But it was more than that. He'd insulted her way of life, everything Gigi had taught her. Her world revolved around sweets, and he'd made it sound so nefarious, so shameful.

Plus, now that she knew the plan for his store, she realized her fears were more than founded—they were far worse than she'd thought.

Sure, his unconventional concept probably wouldn't last in

the long run. It would be a novelty. The locals and tourists would be enamored with its whimsy and charm in the beginning, but the appeal would eventually wear off in favor of comfort and familiarity. But by then, the damage would be done. She could barely last a few more months, even without direct competition next door. With all of her customers flocking to Landon's quirky shop to try the latest craze, she wouldn't stand a chance.

By the time they reached Landon's estate, tears lurked behind her eyelids, threatening to spill out at any moment.

Although Landon lingered as if he wanted to talk and smooth things over, she needed to escape as quickly as possible or risk losing control of her emotions altogether.

With a brusque goodbye, she fled to her truck.

The second her seat belt clicked into place, defeat and disappointment crashed over her.

One tear fell, then another.

Her shoulders trembled, but she refused to let herself cry. Once she opened the floodgates, she'd have to admit another, far more unsettling reason for her crushing disappointment—the foolish, unfounded hope that had snuck into her heart during dinner.

After roughly wiping her tears aside, she slammed the gear shift into drive and put Landon's mansion in her rearview mirror. With any luck, that would be the last time she'd see it.

The entire drive home, she consoled herself with the anticipation of a hot bath and the Agatha Christie novel she'd started the night before. She desperately needed a distraction from the overwhelming weight on her chest.

Sadie bit back a sigh when she spotted the living room light on, realizing Gigi had waited up for her and would want a rundown of the evening.

What could she say? She couldn't admit how close she was to losing everything her grandmother had worked her entire life to build. Nor could she explain how she'd gone from having one of the best nights of her life to one of the most devastating. She could barely admit that difficult truth to herself.

During dinner, she'd seen Landon in a new light—a far more flattering one. She'd been attracted to his playful humor and passion. And witnessing his rapport with his friend Kaito, the respect, admiration, and genuine affection they displayed, not to mention how he'd invested his own money to make the man's dream possible... Well, she'd started to wonder if maybe she'd misjudged him.

But the fleeting illusion had come tumbling down around her, leaving her embarrassed and angry at her own foolishness.

She'd let herself be charmed by Landon once, but never again.

The instant she walked through the front door, her grandmother's Maine coon cats, Truffle and BonBon, coiled around her calves to lend their comforting support.

"Is it that obvious I've had a bad night?" she asked, bending down to give them each a head pat hello.

While most cats got a bad rap for being aloof and self-centered, these two were like doting great-aunts with the occasional mischievous streak, and Sadie loved looking after them while Gigi traveled.

To some, a woman in her late twenties who still lived with her grandmother might be pitiable, but the arrangement suited them. In fact, there were times Sadie wished Gigi traveled less often so they could spend more time together. Although, she'd never admit it. Gigi had already sacrificed over a decade of prime traveling years in order to raise her. Besides, happy single people weren't supposed to be lonely.

She found Gigi in front of the stove in the kitchen, clad in her chenille robe with hot-pink curlers in her hair.

"Just in time, chérie." Gigi poured thick, velvety hot chocolate into two mugs and carried them to the kitchen table, assuming Sadie would join her.

Sadie shrugged out of her coat and hung it on the back of the antique chair before sliding onto the embroidered cushion.

The soothing aroma of dark and white chocolate combined with decadent cream instantly eased some of her tension, just as it had all those years ago the first time Gigi offered her a mug of her painstakingly perfected recipe.

"So, how did it go?" Gigi asked, leaning forward so she didn't miss a word.

Sadie downed a healthy sip of hot chocolate, savoring the silkiness as it warmed her throat. Knowing her grandmother would never let the topic rest without all the details, she spilled the night's events, leaving out the parts about the shop's debt and her momentary lapse in judgment about Landon.

"I don't know what to do," Sadie concluded with a dejected sigh. "What if his new shop hurts business? What if we can't come to a compromise about the booth and I miss my shot to impress the judges? What if—"

"What if the streets flood with marmalade," Gigi finished for her.

"What?" Sadie stared, caught off guard by her absurd statement.

Gigi took a languid sip before lowering the mug, casual as could be. "You're worrying about things that haven't happened yet. That may *never* happen. You're trying to control too much, chérie. You can't catch the rain while it's still in the clouds."

"So, I'm just supposed to do nothing?"

"Not at all," Gigi said with a patient smile. "You focus on what God has already placed in your hands and let Him worry about the rest. And"—her eyes twinkled—"you make chocolate."

Sadie lifted the brim of her mug to her lips to hide their faint quivering as a terrifying thought wormed its way into her already troubled mind.

Make chocolate....

Sure, it sounded simple enough. But what if she couldn't even do that anymore?

Landon crept up the staircase and down the hall, careful not to make a sound. After the night he'd had, the last thing he wanted was to run into his mother or Gladys and be forced to confess how badly he'd blown it with Sadie.

Of course she'd been upset. And he couldn't blame her. He'd come across like a callous jerk. How could he have been so clueless to her feelings?

The more he thought about the evening's fallout, the more his chest ached, as though someone had stomped on it and then twisted their heel for good measure.

He'd have to patch things up with Sadie. But how?

"How was your date?"

His mother's voice caught him by surprise, and he whirled around, spotting her dim outline in the moonlight filtering through the tall stained glass windows.

"It wasn't a date," he muttered, yanking open his bedroom door. "And no offense, Mom, but I'm exhausted and not in the mood to talk." He turned away, hoping she'd take the hint.

"It was that terrible?" she asked, rolling past him without an invitation.

She parked her wheelchair in front of the large stone hearth opposite his custom king-size bed. A flickering fire, courtesy of Gladys, cast a warm amber glow around the spacious master suite, mingling the scent of woodsmoke with expensive leather and the lavender fabric softener Gladys used on his Egyptian cotton sheets.

His haven had just become an interrogation room.

"It could have gone better," he deflected, flicking on the lights.

"What happened?"

Before he had a chance to respond, a sleepy-eyed Reginald padded into the room, not wanting to be left out. He went straight for Irene, who bent down and scooped him into her arms, giving him a loving nuzzle.

Reginald curled into the soft afghan perpetually draped across her lap and leveled his brown eyes on Landon as if to say, *You may continue.*

Landon sighed and slipped out of his blazer. "We don't see eye to eye on a few key areas, which led to a bit of tension during dinner, that's all."

Irene groaned. "You went on your crusade against sugar again, didn't you?"

Landon stiffened at the disapproval in her tone. "Why do you say it like it's a bad thing? I'm trying to help people."

He tossed the blazer on the foot of his bed, frustrated that after all this time, she still couldn't appreciate his efforts. She should understand his motivation better than anyone.

"I know you are," she said, gently this time. "But how did you expect the poor girl to react? She makes candy for a living. You had to know she'd take your position personally."

Landon slumped against the soft mattress, once again faced with his colossal miscalculation of the evening.

He'd been a fool to think one fancy meal and impassioned monologue would sway her to his side. But he'd gotten caught up in the moment, encouraged by how much she'd seemed to be enjoying herself. He'd lost his grip on reality, and he'd hurt her feelings in the process.

"I realize my mistake now."

"So, how are you going to fix it?"

"Honestly, Mom. I have no idea."

CHAPTER 6

Sadie set the plate of chocolate-covered strawberries on the table and joined both of her friends, relieved to take a break from the kitchen and another lackluster batch of bonbons.

"These strawberries look delicious." Lucy helped herself to the biggest one. "Where did you find berries this red in the dead of winter?"

"Are they from our greenhouse?" Olivia asked, selecting a plump berry drizzled with three different types of chocolates and sprinkled with pink sugar.

"Reed dropped them off this morning," Sadie said with a smile. "You two have quite the operation going."

Her friend bit into the ripe, juicy fruit, a blush of pride apparent on her fair complexion.

Olivia Parker moved back to Poppy Creek last spring, giving up a successful event planning business in New York; a bold decision that couldn't have worked out more perfectly. After purchasing a large property next to the flower farm owned by her boyfriend, Reed Hollis, they opened a venue called The Sterling Rose Estate that hosted many of the town's events, including the upcoming Valentine's Day Dance. As if their joint venture wasn't doing well enough, they'd recently added a small berry patch to their endeavors.

Sadie couldn't be happier for her friend and all the professional and personal growth she'd witnessed over the last several months. In fact, she suspected a proposal in the near future.

And Lucy and Vick probably weren't too far behind.

It seemed like all of her childhood friends were happily situated in some state of relational bliss, either married, engaged, or on the brink. And the monogrammed towels, shared dreams, and seamlessly merged lives suited them.

But not everyone wanted the white-picket-fence life or needed constant companionship. She was perfectly content to follow in Gigi's footsteps, living her best life without being tied down to someone else.

Not that her friends ever stopped trying to set her up.

"So, how was your date?" Lucy's blue eyes sparkled with an impish glint.

"It wasn't a date. And even if it had been, there definitely wouldn't be a second one."

"It was that bad?" Olivia wrinkled her nose in sympathy.

"Unless you enjoy being told that your life's passion is detrimental to society." Sadie tried to keep the hurt from her tone, although she couldn't hide the bitter twinge.

"He said that?" Lucy asked in shock.

"Well, he didn't say it about me personally, but it was clearly implied. I still can't believe we have to share a booth at the festival. How am I supposed to occupy the same space as that man?" As she spoke, all of her frustration and anxiety resurfaced, putting a strain on what was supposed to be a nice afternoon break with her friends.

"I'm so sorry, Sadie." Olivia shared a glance with Lucy before adding, "We'd really hoped it would turn out differently."

Before Sadie could remind them—yet again—that Landon was the last man on earth she'd ever consider dating, the bell above the entrance chimed.

A young man in khaki pants and a heavy parka popped inside, out of the cold. For a moment, he merely stood in the doorway, ogling the vast array of sweets, forgetting the enormous bouquet and beautifully wrapped package in his arms.

"Hello, there." Sadie stood and greeted him with a warm smile. "How can I help you?"

He blinked, tearing his gaze from the colorful display cases. "I'm looking for Sadie Hamilton."

"You've found her."

"These are for you." He shoved the package and fragrant floral arrangement into her arms.

"They are?" Surprised, Sadie stared at the gorgeous bundle of blue and white flowers. "Who are they from?"

"I don't know, ma'am. I'm just the courier. Have a nice day."

Before she could press him further, he'd slipped back outside.

Lucy jumped from her seat, eager to ascertain the sender. "Is there a note?"

Sadie gently sifted through the aromatic foliage, then shook her head. "Not that I can see."

"You have a secret admirer!" Lucy squealed, clapping her hands together. "How exciting!"

"Before you start planning our wedding, let's find out who

they're from," Sadie teased, although her heart inexplicably fluttered.

"I recognize the bouquet." Olivia came over for a closer look. "Yep. This is definitely the one Reed made this morning."

"Then you know who sent it?" Landon's name sprang to mind, but Sadie immediately pushed it aside, annoyed that it had entered her subconscious. After all, why would she want him to send her anything?

"Sadly, no. Whoever placed the order did so anonymously through the courier service. But I *can* tell you it's an apology bouquet."

"How do you know that?" Lucy asked.

"Because of the flowers. White orchids, blue hyacinths, and lily of the valley all stand for 'I'm sorry.'"

"How intriguing!" Lucy inched closer and nudged Sadie's shoulder. "Open the package. Maybe there's a note inside."

Her pulse quickening, Sadie carefully set the flowers on the table before tearing into the silver wrapping paper, revealing a white cardboard box. She lifted the lid and brushed aside the thick layers of tissue paper, catching her breath at the unexpected sight tucked underneath.

The photo of her and Gigi holding the Best Local Business award.

Except, the glass had been replaced and the frame had been expertly repaired, cleaned, and polished until it looked brand-new. A single white note card nestled in the lower right corner. The typed font read *An award well-deserved.*

Sadie gaped in disbelief.

An award well-deserved.... What did that mean? Did Landon actually respect the business she'd built despite their conflicting beliefs? Was he extending an olive branch? Or was it some kind of ploy or calculated manipulation? Or something else entirely?

"Well?" Lucy pressed eagerly. "What is it, and what does it all mean?"

"To be honest," Sadie said slowly, fingering the note card. "I'm not sure."

~

Landon knew he should be concentrating on Grant's presentation, but he couldn't stop thinking about Sadie, wondering if she'd received his peace offering yet.

Was his gesture too subtle? Should he have been more direct? How would she react?

As the unanswered questions swirled in his mind, he tapped the side of his ceramic coffee cup, too distracted to appreciate the subtle notes of orange zest and spices in the specialty latte Cassie had created for him when he couldn't decide what to order.

"What's wrong?" Grant asked, pulling Landon from his thoughts. "You don't like the website design?"

A pang of guilt darted through Landon's chest, grounding him in the present. Grant deserved more than his half-hearted attention. And not just because he was the best web designer Landon had ever met. As they'd worked together over the past few years on several business websites, he'd become a good friend. Landon couldn't think of a single person he respected more.

Grant Parker was the kind of man who exuded sincerity, both in his professional and personal life. He was completely without guile and backstabbing ambition, a trait Landon didn't come across often in his typical, power-hungry circles.

It was through his friendship with Grant that he'd fallen for Poppy Creek and decided to pack up everything and relocate, having his mother join him a short time later. If anyone could get through to her, it would be the kindhearted people of this quirky, slightly eccentric town.

If she ever gave them a chance, that is.

"Landon?" Grant pressed, nudging his glasses up the bridge of his nose. "Is everything okay?"

"No. I mean, yes," Landon rambled, once again struggling to focus. "I love the design so far. It's perfect. Sorry, I was lost in thought."

"About?"

"My mom," he confessed, surprised by his own admission. Grant had an uncanny knack for getting him to open up. "We've been living here for a while now, and I can't convince her to leave the house or participate in any of the town's activities."

Grant sipped his cappuccino silently, but his expression spoke volumes.

"What?"

"Nothing." Grant shrugged. "Just that you could stand to be a little more involved in the community yourself."

"What do you mean?" Landon straightened.

For once, Grant was way off base. After all, he was opening a business in the town square, wasn't he? What could be more integrated than that?

"Well, for example, what did you submit for the Saint Valentine Swap?"

"The what?"

"The Saint Valentine Swap. It's like a Secret Santa, but instead of anonymously exchanging gifts, we exchange acts of service." Grant reached into his laptop case and retrieved three cards made out of paper hearts. "Each year, participants fill out one of these valentines with whatever act of service they want to offer and hang it on a garland in the town hall. Then, they randomly choose one for themselves, without peeking inside." Grant explained the unusual tradition as if it was the most normal thing in the world. "This year, Ben's valentine is one week of free yard raking, and Eliza is giving away a private baking class on how to make her famous tiramisu cheesecake. I'm offering a custom pet portrait." To illustrate his point, he showed Landon his red paper heart with navy blue lace around the edges. "See, someone truly immersed in the community would be eager to participate in one of our oldest pastimes, but you'd never even heard of it."

"You're right." Landon sighed. "And I *would* like to participate. But do I have to make my own valentine, or can I buy one?" He side-eyed the frilly paper hearts, not keen on arts and crafts.

"For the pure joy of watching you wield a hot glue gun, I should say that you have to make one, but they have a stack of extras in the town hall." Grant downed the rest of his drink and set the empty cup back on the saucer. "Come on. I'll walk over there with you. Eliza asked me to pin up our valentines since she forgot them at home when she left for work this morning."

Landon finished his latte in a few quick sips and left a generous tip on the table before following Grant outside.

Inside the town hall, Grant led him to the far wall where several garlands stretched across the shiplap siding. They made a festive display of vibrant colors, but Landon hadn't even noticed them when he was here the other night for the meeting. Probably because he'd been too focused on Sadie, not that he cared to admit it.

Grant plucked a pink heart with shimmering gold sequins and glitter from the pile on a nearby table and passed it to him with a grin.

"Seriously?" Landon groaned, frowning at the excessive amount of glitz and sparkle.

"It's either this one or make your own." Grant handed him a pen.

Landon snatched it with a scowl and flipped open the card, but as he stared at the inside fold, his mind went blank. "What should I put? A ride in a private jet? Skybox at Levi's Stadium? Broadway tickets?"

"Whoa! Easy there, Mr. Money Bags," Grant teased. "It doesn't have to be so elaborate or expensive. How about a movie night at your fancy home theater?"

"Really?" Landon frowned. "You don't think that's too simple?"

"Maybe to you. But a lot of people would love to see one of their favorite movies on a screen that size."

Landon twirled the pen, mulling over the suggestion. It wasn't exciting or flashy, but maybe that wasn't the point. He'd trust Grant's instinct. "A movie night it is, then."

He scribbled his offering on the froufrou card and pinned it to the garland while Grant did the same with his family's valentines.

Now, it was time to pick a card for himself. But which one?

As he scanned the available options, his mind wandered to Sadie again. Would she have a valentine somewhere in the gaudy spectacle?

His fingers grazed a red heart with swirling gold glitter. It reminded him of the decorative bows on her chocolate boxes. Curious, he could barely restrain himself from peeking inside.

But purposefully choosing Sadie's valentine was a bad idea. What if she hadn't forgiven him for last night?

His gaze landed on a familiar red heart with blue lace, and he yanked it from the clothespin. His mother would love a custom portrait of Reginald painted by Grant.

And he'd be far better off keeping his distance from Sadie.

CHAPTER 7

Sadie lowered the pretzel ball stuffed with pimento cheese into the bowl of melted milk chocolate, careful to achieve a smooth, even coating. But as she lifted it toward the parchment-lined baking sheet, a cacophonous buzz from a power drill broke her concentration.

Her latest creation slipped from her grasp and plopped onto the counter, squishing into a misshapen mess.

With a whimpering groan, she glowered in the direction of the adjacent wall between her shop and Landon's. Flecks of dust rose into the air as the wall visibly shook.

Worried for their safety, she rushed to relocate the tray of white chocolate bonbons she'd piped full of lemon curd and candied basil earlier that morning.

Although she'd hired Tracey for a few extra hours and confined herself to the kitchen, she still hadn't come up with a prize-winning recipe. She did finally feel like she was on the right track, though. Or, at the very least, she was thinking outside the box a bit more.

Not that it gave her much hope considering she still had to

reach a compromise with Landon over their booth, which seemed impossible.

Her mind drifted to the beautiful bouquet and fully restored picture frame he'd sent over yesterday. And the note.

While part of her wanted to dislike him for the things he'd said, something deep down told her that Landon Morris might be more complicated than she once believed. And she wasn't entirely sure what to do with that realization.

"Hello?"

The loud voice startled Sadie from her thoughts, and she almost dropped the tray of bonbons, barely catching herself in time to set it gently on the opposite counter.

"Sorry." Cassie flashed a sheepish smile as she ducked into the kitchen. "I didn't mean to startle you. Tracey said you'd be back here, and you didn't seem to hear me the first time I called your name."

"No worries. It's not your fault. It's all the construction next door."

"I bet you'll be glad when it's over."

"Yeah..." Sadie said slowly, filled with mixed emotions. On one hand, she couldn't wait for all the commotion to finally quiet down. On the other hand, the end of the renovations would mean Landon's shop would open to the public—a moment she dreaded.

"Eliza sent me to pick up those coffee-infused chocolate chips you made for her," Cassie said, reaching a hand inside the front pocket of her apron. "She also asked me to give you this."

Sadie stared at the pink construction heart in Cassie's hand, vaguely recalling how Eliza had offered to take care of her valentine for her since she'd been so busy lately. "Oh, right. Thanks. I'd forgotten all about the Saint Valentine Swap. I've been so focused on the contest entry."

"How's it going?" Cassie scanned the clutter of ingredients strewn about the kitchen.

"Great," she lied, wincing as the accusing *thwack* of a hammer called her bluff. "Truthfully, it could be going better," she admitted with a sigh.

"What's wrong?"

"I've made dozens and dozens of chocolates, taking more creative risks with each one, but nothing feels… right."

Cassie's features softened as she glanced at a bar of dark chocolate filled with pine nuts and capers. Admittedly, not Sadie's finest flavor combination.

"Is it possible you're trying too hard?" Cassie asked kindly. "Maybe the answer is simpler than you think."

"Maybe." Sadie forced a smile, though her usually astute friend couldn't be more wrong this time. *Simple* was the exact opposite of what she needed.

"Well, don't worry. You'll come up with something perfect."

An electric saw joined the chaotic chorus of the power drill and hammer, raising the volume to near deafening levels.

Cassie offered a sympathetic grimace. "Guess I should let you get back to work."

"Yes, escape while you can," Sadie teased.

When Cassie disappeared through the swinging door, Sadie turned toward the rattling wall, both hands on her hips.

This was getting ridiculous. Loose plaster crumbled from the ceiling and the wall appeared to bow. *Yeesh.* Were they trying to break through to the other side?

As if in response to her unasked question, a sizable crack

zig-zagged up the drywall, followed by a startling crash as a huge chunk separated and clattered onto the countertop.

Landon jerked his attention from the foreman as shouts erupted from the other side of the room. One of the crew members swatted at a cloud of dust hovering in front of his face, coughing beneath his safety mask, while the other men gathered around to assess the situation.

As the dust settled, Landon's heart slammed against his chest.

A gaping hole loomed in the center of the wall.

Sadie's horrified expression gazed back at him, perfectly in frame.

Great. Just great.

If she didn't loathe him before, this would definitely push her over the edge.

He strode across the room and addressed the workman. "What happened?"

"I—I'm sorry, sir," the flustered twentysomething stammered, removing his mask and safety glasses. "According to the original blueprint, there's supposed to be a support beam here."

"Are you sure?"

"I—I think so. I'll check." He shuffled toward the workstation, leaving Landon to smooth things over with Sadie.

He cleared his throat. "I'm really sorry about this. I'll have them patch it up immediately."

"How long do you think it will take?"

"A few hours. I'll have them stop everything else and make

it a priority. Was anything else damaged? If so, I'll have it fixed or replaced."

"I don't think so. Luckily, I'd moved the chocolates right before." Her gaze flitted across the pile of debris on the countertop, and he wondered why she was being so nice about the whole thing. They'd clearly made a mess of her kitchen and she had every right to be upset.

"Again, I'm really sorry," he reiterated. "The guys are normally incredibly thorough. If they thought there was a support beam here, something must be wrong with the plans." He stepped closer to inspect the hole, and a glimmer of light reflected off something metallic, catching his eye.

"What was that?" Sadie asked, leaning forward.

She must have seen the same glint.

"I'm not sure." He removed a lump of plaster, revealing a rectangular tin wedged inside the wall.

"What in the world?" Her hazel eyes widened with interest, and she gingerly lifted the object from its hiding spot. "It's beautiful," she breathed, brushing a layer of dust from the hand-painted lid that depicted a faded image of the Eiffel Tower surrounded by cherry blossoms. Based on the tarnished metal and chipped paint, the box had been enclosed in the wall for decades, if not longer.

"What is it?" His own curiosity piqued, he waited for Sadie to pry back the lid, which had warped over time.

"It's a box of letters." She stared at the stack of yellowed pages covered in sloping script.

"What kind of letters?"

"I'm not sure." She turned one over, a crease appearing in her brow. "That's odd. They're in French."

"That is strange." Why would old letters written in a foreign language be stuffed inside a wall in Poppy Creek? "I studied French for a few semesters in college. I'm a little rusty, but I can try to translate them."

"Thanks, but my grandmother is fluent." She replaced the lid. "I'll take them over to her while your men patch up the wall."

"Sure. I'll have them start on it right now."

With a brief nod of acknowledgment, she turned away, then paused, swiveling back around to face him. "Thank you for the flowers. And for fixing the frame."

Her tense body language hinted at her discomfort, as though she wasn't quite sure what to make of him. Or his gesture.

Fair enough. He wasn't entirely sure what to make of the situation, either.

On one hand, he found himself strangely interested in spending more time with her. On the other hand, he couldn't think of a more dangerous proposition.

CHAPTER 8

"You'll never guess what I found!" Sadie shouted breathlessly as she burst into the living room.

Gigi looked up from the card table strewn with travel brochures and a creased map of Estonia, her next adventure destination. "Clearly something important enough to pull you away from work in the middle of the day." A teasing smile played about her crimson lips, and she leaned back in the plush recliner, giving Sadie her full attention.

"Tracey is covering for me, thankfully, because I couldn't wait to show you this." She squished onto the couch beside Truffle and BonBon, who batted a tangled ball of yarn between them. "I found this hidden in one of the walls at the shop." Barely able to contain her excitement, she set the metal box on the pile of loose papers.

A flicker of surprise darted across Gigi's face. "In the wall?"

"It's a long story. But wait until you see what's inside." Sadie leaned forward, her elbows propped on her knees, as Gigi carefully pried open the lid.

"Letters," her grandmother murmured, staring at the faded ink and crinkled pages.

"Not just any letters." Sadie inched forward, teetering on the edge of the cushion. "*Secret* letters hidden away for decades." She paused for dramatic effect before adding, "And they're in French."

"French?" Gigi repeated. Apparently, she'd been stunned into one-word sentences.

Sadie grinned. It took a lot to render her grandmother speechless.

After all the *Murder, She Wrote* episodes and Agatha Christie adaptations they'd watched over the years, she would enjoy solving the mystery together. "I can only make out a few words, but they appear to be love letters between two people named Abélard and Lise. Will you translate them for me?"

Gigi sat in silence for a few moments before replacing the lid. "I don't think so, chérie."

"Really?" Sadie straightened, accidentally knocking the ball of yarn off the couch.

With a flick of her tail, Truffle bounded after it, followed by BonBon, who didn't want to be left out of the fun new game.

"Why not?" Sadie asked, stunned her grandmother would pass up an opportunity to employ her sleuthing skills.

"Seems to me, if someone went through all the trouble of hiding these letters in the wall, they didn't want them found." She handed Sadie the box and turned her attention to an article she'd printed off the internet titled "Skydive Estonia."

Dumbfounded, Sadie glanced from her grandmother to the letters in her lap, trying to piece together what had just happened. She supposed Gigi had a point. Reading the letters *would* be an invasion of privacy. But they were ancient.

Possibly even historic. Wasn't there a statute of limitations on reading old love letters?

A small voice in the back of her mind said she should follow her grandmother's advice and put the box back where she found it. She certainly didn't need a distraction, especially with the competition right around the corner.

But something about the letters and their clandestine location tugged at her sense of curiosity and wouldn't let go.

She needed to know what they said.

And considering Gigi constantly bemoaned the inaccuracy of online translators when it came to the delicate nuances of the French language, she knew only one other person who might be able to help her.

But could she bring herself to ask him?

~

Landon drew in a deep breath and pushed through the front door of Sadie's Sweet Shop. A bell chimed overhead, welcoming him inside along with the overwhelming scent of rich chocolate and confectioners' sugar, as though he were any other candy-loving customer.

For a moment, he couldn't move, struck by the reality that he'd never set foot inside her shop before, and he wasn't sure how to feel about it. In some ways, it felt like crossing enemy lines.

"Hi." A young girl with hair the color of candied lime greeted him with a look of surprise. To her credit, she recovered from her shock quickly enough to offer him a smile. "What can I help you with today?"

"I was hoping to inspect the hole my men repaired, to make sure they fixed everything to your satisfaction."

"Oh. Well, Sadie isn't here right now, but I can show you, if you'd like."

"That'd be great, thanks." Suppressing the twinge of disappointment that he wouldn't see Sadie, he stepped behind the counter and followed her to the kitchen in back.

An assortment of chocolates and haphazard supplies covered every inch of the stainless steel countertops, catching him off guard.

"Excuse the mess." She waved a hand, encompassing the clutter. "Sadie's been working nonstop on a new recipe for the Tastiest Treat competition."

"The contest must be important to her." Landon surveyed the disarray with new eyes, marveling at the amount of work she'd put into it.

"Oh, yes. It always is. Although, this year she seems extra intent on winning, for some reason."

Landon let this information sink in, wondering if he had anything to do with her increased motivation. "What about you? Are you a chocolatier as well?"

The girl blushed, appearing pleased that he'd asked. "Sadie is teaching me. She says I have a real knack for it, but I don't think my parents would be happy if I gave up college to pursue candy making, even if I would love to open my own store one day. It was hard enough to get them to agree to my gap year after high school."

"You could always get a business degree. I'm sure it takes a lot of management and marketing skills to run a shop like this." Landon blinked, taken aback by his own words. Was he really encouraging this girl to pursue a career in confections? He should be steering her toward a different vocation. *Any* vocation other than this one.

"You know, that's not a bad idea." Her brow furrowed as she mulled over his suggestion.

Backpedaling, he added, "Of course, there's a lot you can do with a business degree, if you change your mind about owning a candy store."

"Oh, I don't think I'll change my mind." Her contemplative expression instantly morphed into a bright, bubbly smile. "Ever since I first set foot in this place and met Sadie, I knew I wanted the same career when I grew up."

"Why's that?" Landon had forgotten all about the repaired hole in the wall, keenly interested in what she had to say.

"Because it's the coolest job in the world," she said with matter-of-fact sincerity. "Sadie makes people happy for a living. Every day, I either see someone walk in here with a smile and leave with an even bigger one. Or they come in sad or melancholy and completely transform by the time they walk out. It's like magic."

"Magic, huh?" He couldn't help noting he'd used the same word to describe molecular gastronomy to Sadie.

"I know it's cheesy." She shrugged, her cheeks tinged pink with another self-conscious blush. "But I'd love to make that kind of impact on someone. The way Sadie does." Her gaze fluttered to the ground, and she murmured, "Sorry. This all probably sounds really silly to you."

As he saw himself through the lens of this sweet, hopeful teenager, an unpleasant realization washed over him.

His vehement antisugar reputation—all the impassioned interviews, TV appearances, and public statements he'd made over the past year, not to mention the campaigns and organizations he'd vocally supported—had made an impression.

And he got the feeling it wasn't a good one.

As his mother described it, he'd taken it upon himself to launch a crusade.

Was he taking things too far?

Or not far enough?

And how could he be sure either way?

CHAPTER 9

Sadie placed the tip of her finger on the doorbell, then hesitated, curling it back.

Should she really go through with this? Did she need to know what the letters said badly enough to ask Landon Morris for help?

The metal box in her purse suddenly felt heavier, straining on her shoulder as if encouraging her to carry on with the plan.

Sucking in a breath, she forced herself to press the bell, flinching as the musical chime signaled that it was too late to turn back now.

"Why, hello, dear." Gladys beamed at her from the doorway. "It's Sadie, right?"

"Yes. It's nice to see you again." Some of Sadie's nerves relaxed at the woman's friendly smile. "I'm here to see Landon, if he's available."

"You know, I haven't seen him all day, but he's usually home by now." Gladys stepped to the side, holding the door open a bit wider. "Why don't you come inside, and I'll see if I can find him."

"Thank you." Sadie followed her into the foyer, hugging her purse closer to her side.

The letters. You're here because of the letters.

"I'll have you wait in the den while I track him down." Gladys tugged open a pair of French doors, revealing a cozy sitting room with plush furniture and built-in bookcases flanking a large stone hearth. "There's a nice, warm fire and a beverage cart in the corner, so make yourself comfortable. I may be a few minutes."

"Thanks so much."

When Gladys left, Sadie stood stiffly in the center of the room, hyperaware that she was inhabiting Landon's space. This was his furniture, where he sat enjoying the firelight, probably reading one of the many books that filled the solid oak shelves.

Curious about his literary tastes, she wandered toward the far shelf and studied the titles, finding a mix of contemporary and classics. When she caught sight of the soft leather binding of *The Secret Garden*, her heart thrummed. She'd adored the story as a child, poring over the pages of her well-loved copy until they'd started falling out.

The one in Landon's collection appeared to be an early edition, and she couldn't resist sliding it off the shelf for a closer look.

As she slipped it from its resting spot, a subtle *click* emanated from somewhere inside the wooden panel behind it, followed by a creaking sound.

Astonished, Sadie gaped as the entire bookcase swung open, revealing a hidden doorway.

For several seconds, she stood frozen in disbelief. She'd

seen secret passageways in movies but didn't think they existed in real life. At least, not in ordinary life. But then, Landon Morris wasn't ordinary, was he?

Inching forward, she peered through the dimly lit ingress, noting a faint glow on the other side. Her pulse hammered in her ears as she took one step, then another, uncertain what lay ahead.

When she reached the end of the tunnel, the scent of aged leather and, strangely, the earthiness of the outdoors greeted her. Her eyes adjusted to the shift in brightness, widening when the room came into focus.

That is, if one could call the space something as prosaic as a *room*.

One half resembled a library worthy of Belle in *Beauty and the Beast*—three stories of gleaming bookshelves overflowing with more books than one person could read in a lifetime. The other half reminded her of Reed Hollis's Victorian greenhouse with its wrought iron and glass walls encompassing dozens of lush plants and a magnificent water feature.

Sadie could only imagine the ingenuity—not to mention the electricity bill—required to regulate the climate for such different environments rolled into one seamless space. But she supposed if anyone could make it work, it would be a billionaire like Landon.

What caught her eye the most was an intricate elevator system that traveled the length and height of the bookshelves. It seemed like pure decadence in conjunction with the sliding ladders and spiral staircases, but someone like Landon could afford to satisfy every whim.

Her thoughts flickered to the ramp out front, sparking more questions than answers. Was it luxury for luxury's sake? Or something more?

She moved farther into the room, pausing at the sound of crackling logs.

Naively, she'd assumed she was alone.

Her pulse quickened as her gaze fell on an older woman—maybe late fifties, early sixties—reading in front of the fire, a ball of chocolate-brown fur curled in her lap.

In one sweeping glance, Sadie clocked the same dark hair and strong yet refined features as Landon.

The woman was undoubtedly beautiful.

She was also in a wheelchair, her lower half shrouded in a heavy afghan.

As if sensing her presence, the little dog lifted its head, emitting a low, protective growl when it spotted her.

The woman glanced up from her book, surprise, confusion, then curiosity crossing her countenance in rapid succession.

"You must be Sadie." She scratched behind the dog's ear and the growling ceased, replaced by a look of pure contentment.

"Yes, but how did you know that?" Sadie was positive she'd never met, or even seen, this woman before.

"I can see why my son is taken with you. Please, have a seat." She waved toward the brocade armchair opposite her by the fire.

But Sadie couldn't move, too stunned by the woman's words. *Son. Taken with you*. Had she misheard?

"Reginald won't bite." She smiled this time, though it didn't reach her eyes.

"You're Landon's mother?" Sadie said slowly, sinking onto the chair. She'd heard a rumor that Landon's mother had moved in with him, but she'd never caught so much as a single glimpse of her. Eventually, she'd assumed the rumor was unfounded.

"Please, call me Irene. Are you here to see my son?"

"Yes, I was waiting in the den when I accidentally stumbled across the secret passageway."

"Aren't those fun? There are a few of them around the house. They were here when Landon bought the place. The previous owners were quite eccentric, but I rather love all the quirks."

"Is that why you never leave?" Sadie asked without thinking. She blushed, adding, "I'm sorry. It's just that I've never seen you around town before."

"Don't apologize. I like a woman who can speak her mind. I'm sure that's one of the many things Landon likes about you, too."

Sadie's blush deepened. She didn't have the heart to tell the woman she was sorely mistaken. Why tell someone that you and their offspring don't get along?

"To answer your question," Irene continued. "Yes, that's part of the reason. I'm also not very social and prefer to spend time with my books."

"Does that ever get lonely?"

Irene didn't answer right away, the silence heightened by a snapping log in the fire.

"What are you here to see Landon about?" Irene asked instead, avoiding her question.

Sadie shifted on the soft cushion, not sure how to respond. "Well… I, uh, need to ask him a favor."

"How interesting." Irene's eyes brightened. "You'll have to tell me all about it over dinner."

"Dinner?"

"You'll join us, of course. It'll be ready shortly. I'll tell

Gladys to set an extra plate for you. Besides, she's probably wondering where you wandered off to." Irene cradled Reginald securely in her lap before switching on her mechanical wheelchair. "Come along."

Sadie scrambled to her feet, too stunned to speak.

Dinner? With Landon and his mother?

This evening wasn't turning out at all how she'd expected.

But she had a feeling Irene wouldn't take no for an answer.

And, if she were honest, she wanted to see what other surprises the evening might uncover.

Landon could barely taste the bite of garlic and rosemary chicken, too flummoxed by the sight of his mother and Sadie conversing at the other end of the table.

His mother notoriously refused to have company over. Why had she suddenly made an exception?

Not only had she invited Sadie to stay for dinner, she seemed to be enjoying herself. Was it possible that Sadie, of all people, would be the one to draw his mother out of her seclusion?

Warmth spread across his chest as Sadie said something that made his mother laugh—genuinely laugh.

She truly was something special, wasn't she?

All night, he could barely take his eyes off her, noticing each infinitesimal detail, like the silky strands of hair that had escaped her ponytail, framing her face. His fingers itched to remove the elastic band and watch it spill around her shoulders.

Although she didn't possess the soft, symmetrical features most of society touted as ideal, she stood out in a sea of sameness. From the moment they met, he recognized a woman of substance with the kind of striking beauty that radiated from the inside out.

While his heart longed to explore the possibilities, his mind couldn't reconcile their differences. Even if she was interested—which she clearly wasn't—they'd be doomed before they ever began.

He cleared his throat, dismissing his conflicted thoughts. "You said you needed to ask me a favor?"

"Yes." Sadie set down her fork and turned to face him. "Those letters we found earlier... do you think you could translate them after all?"

"Sure. Like I said, I'm rusty, and it might take me a while, but I'll give it my best shot."

"Letters?" Irene asked.

"We found them hidden inside the wall between our two shops," Sadie explained. "They're written in French, so I only recognize a few words, but they appear to be love letters."

"How mysterious! And romantic. Like something you'd read about in a novel."

Uh-oh. Landon hoped his mother wasn't getting any more ideas about him and Sadie and hopeless happy endings.

"I'd really love to find out who they belong to," Sadie confessed. "Maybe they'd like to have them back after all these years."

"You must be a romantic at heart," Irene noted, appearing pleased by the observation.

"Not really. I mean, 'happily ever after' is fine for some people. But not everyone. Some people are better off alone."

"Absolutely," Irene agreed. "But I don't think you're one of those people."

Sadie blushed, looking decidedly uncomfortable.

Landon scowled at his mother above the rim of his water glass, though she didn't seem to notice. Or more likely, chose to ignore him.

While she spent most of her time alone, surely she hadn't forgotten basic social etiquette.

A long, awkward silence ensued, slightly alleviated by Reggie's loud chewing.

"Reginald is one lucky pup," Sadie said, graciously switching subjects.

Landon followed her gaze. The spoiled canine gobbled up a bowl of gourmet food, not so unlike their own.

"I've never really bought into the myth that dogs need to eat dry kibble," Irene admitted. "As a vet, I've seen dramatic health benefits from feeding them a balanced and nutrient-dense diet of real, natural ingredients."

"You're a vet?"

Irene blinked, as though she'd just realized what she'd said.

Landon's muscles tensed, and he watched his mother closely.

She never talked about the past, to the point of being worrisome. When he'd offered to pay for a prestigious psychologist in the city, she'd stubbornly refused, even as her despondency toward life grew worse.

She'd been responding so well to Sadie up until now, he prayed this didn't ruin her progress.

"I used to be," she said softly, staring at her plate.

"What a fascinating job. What kinds of animals did you treat?" Sadie took a sip of water, either not recognizing the shift in her demeanor or choosing to overlook it.

Landon suppressed a smile, grateful for her persistence.

"Dogs and cats, mostly. But I was trained to treat a wide variety of animals, including the occasional exotic pet. Even a few livestock, which was interesting." Her gaze softened, burnished with the warmth of a fond memory.

Landon's chest ached, regret washing over him. If only he could go back in time and do things differently. If only he'd noticed what was happening; if he could have done something sooner to prevent...

He gulped his ice water, dispelling the unwelcome—and unhelpful—thoughts.

"You must have the best stories," Sadie said, sounding genuinely interested. "I'd love to hear them."

"Maybe some other time." His mother smiled again, but the light had vanished from her eyes, replaced by their usual dull sheen—the dim, lifeless glaze that meant she'd retreated into her fortress of isolation.

The one he couldn't rescue her from, no matter how hard he tried.

CHAPTER 10

The next morning, Landon awoke facedown on his desk. Groggy and sore from his prolonged hunched position, he lifted his head, a sheet of paper clinging to his cheek.

He brushed it aside then ran a hand over the back of his stiff neck, massaging the tight muscles in slow circles as the events of last night came into focus.

Miraculously, he'd spent an enjoyable evening with Sadie and his mother, which felt more like a dream than a reality. After Sadie left, he'd taken the box of letters to his room and worked on translating the first one.

The letter!

A tiny jolt darted through his chest at the memory; the private words stealing back into his mind.

While he'd taken some liberties, translating certain romanticisms into more recognizable American expressions, the gist of the letter remained clear. And something about rewriting the letter in his own hand, with the intent of then passing it along to Sadie, made him feel vulnerable and exposed.

He turned the paper over and scanned his measured handwriting, wondering if the words were as intimate as he remembered.

My Dearest Lise,

Although we haven't known each other for long, you've already captured my heart completely. Despite our differences, I'm drawn to you as I've never been drawn to anyone before.

There's a connection between us. One that defies reason and logic. It transcends common sense and even chemistry. It's magic. An inexplicable spark that makes two people, who couldn't be more different, bring out the best in each other. Who are we to deny such a spark or try to snuff it out? If anything, we should fan the flame.

But I can't do it alone.

Come back to me, my love.

The world has lost all color without you.

Faithfully,

Your Abélard

Something about the man's sincere and fervent—if a smidge sappy—sentiments touched a place in Landon's heart he'd been trying to ignore.

Similar to finding love in unlikely places, many of the world's most notable advances in science happened by accident. Or at least, the outcome was different than the original intent, like Percy Spencer's failed attempt to create an energy source for radar equipment that led to the invention of the microwave.

In science, the pursuit of the truth was paramount, even if the findings disproved the original hypothesis.

By denying the result, no matter how startling and unexpected, could something wonderful—maybe even life-altering—be extinguished?

And at what cost?

A knock at the door yanked him from his thoughts. "Come in." He quickly stacked the letters and stuffed them inside the tin as though hiding a private journal.

Gladys swept into the room brandishing his favorite running shoes. "I've taken the liberty of giving them a good polish for the race today."

Landon hid a smile. "You realize they're just going to get dirty again?"

"That may be so. But no one in my care is waltzing around town in a pair of scuffed sneakers."

He wasn't sure he'd call a three-mile obstacle course consisting of mud pits and monkey bars *waltzing,* but he appreciated her motherly care. "With shoes this shiny, how can I lose?"

She pursed her lips in playful amusement, then asked, "Why do they call the race the Cupid Run?"

"I'm not sure you'd believe me if I told you." He'd barely believed it himself when Grant explained the quirky tradition as part of his mission to get Landon more involved in the community.

But then, nothing in Poppy Creek should surprise him anymore.

Never able to stay idle for long, Gladys plumped the suede throw pillows on the leather lounge in front of the fireplace, waiting for his explanation.

"The event, which raises awareness for cardiovascular disease, has a Valentine's Day theme," he told her. "Near the end of the race, volunteers dressed like Cupid tag runners with NERF arrows that explode with colored chalk dust on contact. The last obstacle requires teamwork to complete. And you can only partner with someone marked with the same color chalk."

Midfluff, Gladys stared at him in wide-eyed bemusement.

Landon chuckled. "See, I knew you wouldn't believe me."

"And this is supposed to be fun?" she asked, struggling to grasp the concept.

"Loads of fun. Especially if you win." Although there wasn't a prize, per se, the winner earned the seat of honor at the pancake breakfast following the race. Not to mention bragging rights and all the crispy bacon a guy could eat. Or *girl*.

While he suspected Jack Gardener and Colt Davis would be his toughest competition, he'd heard Sadie could hold her own.

A quick image flashed into his mind of Sadie bursting past him at the finish line, covered in mud, her face beaming in triumph.

Although an attractive image, he didn't intend to lose.

Not even to a formidable force like Sadie Hamilton.

As Sadie tied her cleats—twisting the laces into a double knot for good measure—she kept a close eye on Landon. He leaned into a forward lunge just behind the starting line, bantering with Jack and Colt about who'd finish first.

All three men stood over six feet tall, with broad shoulders and the kind of muscles that could stretch a T-shirt. But what she lacked in rippling six packs, she made up for with agility. And stubborn determination.

"Are you ladies ready?" Eliza bounced on her toes, swinging both arms to get her blood flowing in the chilly air. She looked adorable in hot-pink compression pants and a matching tank top.

"Ready as I'll ever be." Lucy's teeth chattered despite her designer hoodie and glittery spandex.

Both women could be an advertisement for stylish activewear, while Sadie's black leggings and faded sweatshirt could be the before photo of a much-needed makeover. But they'd all look the same caked in mud.

She slid her gaze back to Landon, startled to find him staring in her direction. Her cheeks flushed despite herself, and she quickly looked away, irked by the flutter in her stomach.

Grabbing her ankle from behind, she stretched her hamstring, ignoring the warmth that crept across her skin. Ever since dinner with Landon and his mother, her emotions pinged back and forth like a pinball machine, leaving her conflicted and confused.

On one hand, she admired the way he doted on his mother, clearly a protective and caring son. She'd long believed you could tell the most about a person by how they treated others, and her recent observations of Landon—both at the restaurant in the city and at his home—didn't align with her initial impression.

Which bothered her more than she cared to admit.

Truthfully, she didn't *want* to like him.

Life was simpler when she could squeeze him into the cookie-cutter mold of the man who wanted to abolish sugar—and put her out of business.

How could she reconcile that man with the one she'd come to know over the last several days? She couldn't. And it was driving her to distraction.

"Good luck, ladies!" Cassie called out, interrupting her thoughts.

Cassie and Olivia looked like quite the pair in all white workout clothes and feathery wings, which offered a comical contrast to the plastic bows and arrows befitting a child's toy arsenal.

"Catch us if you can," Eliza shouted back playfully.

"You can't outrun love!" Cassie waved one of the arrows, flinging red chalk dust in the air.

Was it Sadie's imagination or did she wink at her?

With a mental shrug, she joined the throng of runners as Mayor Burns called everyone to the starting line. Up ahead, Jack and Colt elbowed each other in the ribs, goading one another with good-natured insults. She rolled her eyes. *Boys.* Fixing her gaze on the first obstacle, she inhaled deeply, then released one slow breath.

Focus. Don't let them get inside your head.

With the bang of a starter pistol, the mass of bodies surged forward, making their way to the climbing cargo net. Tuning out her competitors, Sadie grabbed the thick, vertical rope and placed her foot in the crook of the knot, pressing outward to tighten the net. She repeated the motion, traversing the web with speed and precision.

As she completed each subsequent obstacle, from the mud pit to the army crawl, she moved farther ahead of the pack. Besides the physical endurance, it took all of her willpower not to be on a constant lookout for Landon. The distraction would only slow her down.

After tackling the balance beam, she spotted a row of

narrow tubes. She didn't think twice before wriggling inside the nearest one, inching across the slick surface like a banana slug. She exited on all fours, her gaze fixed on the obstacle ahead.

The *last* obstacle.

A towering wall too tall for any one individual to scale on their own.

"Shoot. You're the wrong color." Colt, the only other runner in sight, huffed in disappointment. He angled his body, showcasing his entire backside covered in blue chalk dust.

Sadie stood, wiping her muddy hands on her equally grimy thighs, smearing the red powder decorating her lower half. The first one to secure a partner would have a fifty-fifty shot at victory.

Jack shimmied out of the tube next, his bulky frame barely making it through the slim passageway. Sadie's pulse spiked in anticipation, but the green chalk coating his face and torso wasn't a match, either.

"Oh, great," Colt muttered. "It's the Jolly Green Giant."

Ignoring him, Jack tossed Sadie a grin. "Looks like we get a live performance from the Blue Man Group while we wait."

Entertained by their friendly bickering, Sadie laughed, but it died in her throat when a large hand grabbed the end of the pipe. They each held their breath, anxiously awaiting a glimpse of telltale dust.

As the runner crawled forward, Sadie's heart leaped at the sight of red chalk spackling the muscled forearm.

But who was it? Luke? Reed? Grant? She couldn't tell.

Her heart skidded to a halt when Landon slithered out of the opening.

Jack and Colt shared a collective groan.

"Nice to see you guys, too," Landon teased.

Nearly every inch of his athletic frame was coated in mud, as though he'd been dunked in dark chocolate then sprinkled with red powdered sugar. And she hated to admit it, but it wasn't a bad look on him.

"We don't have much time." He strode to the wall. "Luke was right behind me." After a quick assessment, he said, "You give me a boost, then I'll pull you up."

She hesitated. What would stop him from ditching her at the top?

"Sadie? Are you ready?"

Uncertain, she met his gaze. His deep-brown eyes held hers. She didn't detect any deception, but how could she be sure?

"Finally!" Colt cheered when his brother, Luke, squirmed into view, his upper body tinted blue.

It was now or never. But she couldn't budge.

"Sadie," Landon said again, softer this time, more focused and intentional. "You have to trust me."

He was right. They couldn't swap roles. While she was strong enough to give him a leg up, she'd never be able to lift his body weight.

With a resigned sigh, she dropped to one knee and threaded her fingers, creating a step with her palms. "Let's do this."

Landon grinned, situating his heel in her hands. In the span of a single breath, he scaled the wall.

Time for the moment of truth.

Chewing her bottom lip, she watched him toss his legs over the other side.

Her pulse faltered. He was going to leave her standing there. She knew it! Why had she fallen for his "trust me" line?

Beside her, Colt and Luke prepared to follow their lead, while Jack whooped when Reed emerged dappled in green.

Like a fool, she'd be left to wait for another red-tinted runner while they all crossed the finish line. Behind Landon.

She shot a glare up the wall, shocked to find him leaning over the edge, reaching for her.

"Come on, Sade. Second place is calling your name."

Sade… Only Lucy used that nickname. The sound made her stomach spin.

Without thinking, she vaulted off the ground, grasping his hand.

His strong grip sent a strange current rippling up her arm, but she blamed it on adrenaline.

Focus on the finish line. The end goal. Don't get distracted.

And whatever you do, don't fall for Landon Morris.

CHAPTER 11

Landon let go of the wall, landing in the soft earth on the other side.

In a daze, he couldn't move. Couldn't think.

During the brief moment their hands met, a spark jolted through his fingertips, like touching a live wire.

Had Sadie felt it, too?

Suddenly, the world came back into focus as mud splattered against his calves. From Sadie's cleats. As she sprinted toward the finish line.

Coming to his senses, he darted after her.

Every muscle in his body screamed as he pushed himself harder, fighting to catch up. Man was she fast.

Winded, he crossed the finish line a millisecond too late. But to his surprise, the expected disappointment never came. He couldn't tear his gaze from her face, mesmerized by the happy glow. Lost in the sight, he stood there staring for an indeterminable amount of time, marveling at her beauty unmarred by the thick layers of mud.

Go over there. Congratulate her. Shake her hand.

Her hand.... At the thought, his fingers involuntarily flexed, recalling the feel of her. Somehow, they seemed to fit together like pieces of a puzzle. Like one of those artsy, mind-bending puzzles that defied logic.

"You should go over there." Appearing out of nowhere, Grant nudged his shoulder, following his gaze to where Sadie stood, surrounded by fellow runners offering their congratulations.

"Why would I do that?"

"How about to prove you're not a sore loser?" Something in Grant's teasing tone hinted at an entirely different motivation than friendly sportsmanship.

"Nah. I'm good."

He needed to keep his distance from Sadie as much as possible.

If only to hide his growing feelings that were becoming dangerously transparent.

~

The next day, Sadie couldn't stop thinking about the race. Or the feel of her hand firmly clasped in Landon's.

Why had her body reacted to the fleeting contact? She certainly didn't like him. Far from it. So, why had her insides turned to mush at his touch?

"Sadie."

She jumped at Tracey's voice over her shoulder and drew in a sharp breath.

"Sorry, I didn't mean to startle you."

"It's okay. I'm skittish these days." She tried to laugh it off, silently chiding herself for being preoccupied by thoughts of

Landon. "What's up?"

"I forgot to tell you I found this when I was cleaning the kitchen last night." Tracey handed her a pink valentine adorned with gold sequins and glitter.

"Thanks. I'd forgotten all about it." Just like she'd forgotten so many things these days, torn between her anxiety about her shop and dwelling on a certain someone she really shouldn't be thinking about at all.

"What'd you get for the Saint Valentine Swap?" Tracey asked. "I got a knitting lesson with Dolores Whittaker."

"Lucky!" Sadie smiled. "You'll love spending time with her." She flipped open the paper heart and her smile instantly faded.

"What's wrong? All the color just drained from your face."

Unable to answer, Sadie stared at the neat, even print, her throat dry.

"What is it? What could be so bad?" Tracey held out her hand.

Flustered, Sadie passed her the card.

Tracey's silver-blue eyes doubled in disbelief. "A movie night with Landon Morris?"

"Wait! Did it say *with*?" Sadie's voice squeaked. "It's at his house, but it didn't say *with*, did it?"

Unbidden, a vision of the two of them curled up on a cozy couch darted through her mind. Her cheeks heated, and she thanked the heavens Tracey couldn't read her thoughts.

"You're right. It doesn't specify that you have to watch it together, but—" Before Tracey could finish her sentence, the bell above the front door jingled. "Be right back."

Tracey returned the card before leaving the kitchen to assist the customer.

As if it had scorched her fingers, Sadie flung the valentine onto the counter and strode to the sink for a cool glass of water. She chugged it down, but the stifling air still compressed around her.

Maybe she could swap valentines with someone else? Normally, that was against the rules, but she'd seen way too much of Landon lately. And given the way her traitorous hormones kept acting up against her will, it wasn't wise to spend more time with him than was absolutely necessary. And a movie night definitely wasn't necessary.

How had this happened, anyway? The odds were remarkably low that she'd choose his valentine when there were—

Her hand froze, the glass poised halfway to her lips as a thought struck her.

Eliza had picked it out! Would her matchmaking friend have stooped to rigging the system in order to get them together? Sadie snorted at her own question. She certainly wouldn't put it past her.

With a defeated groan, she gulped the last drop of water, nearly dropping the glass when someone cleared their throat behind her.

She turned, every nerve in her body going rigid at the sight of Landon.

"Sorry. Your employee... Tracey, I believe... said I'd find you back here." He brandished a folded sheet of paper. "I translated the first letter."

Before she could speak, his gaze landed on the pink-and-gold heart burning a hole through the stainless steel countertop.

The reality of the situation registered on his face. "Is that mine?"

Struggling to swallow, Sadie nodded.

What would he say? Would he be as uncomfortable with the situation as she was?

To her surprise, a slow smile spread across his face. "Do you know what movie you'd like to watch?"

"No. I, uh, haven't given it much thought yet."

"Well, what's your favorite movie?"

"*You've Got Mail*," she blurted on impulse, then immediately regretted it.

"That's a romantic comedy, right? With Tom Hanks?"

"Uh-huh." Why, oh why had she opened her mouth? She didn't want to watch *any* movie with Landon, let alone a romantic one.

"Perfect. I like Tom Hanks, and I haven't seen that one."

Great. She'd really dug her own grave this time.

"What's it about?"

"It's... um..." she stammered, coming up blank.

He cocked his head to the side, appearing amused by her sudden loss for words.

Her already flushed cheeks were smoldering now. "To be honest, I don't remember."

"But it's your favorite?" His smile grew to a full-on grin, and she couldn't be more mortified.

"Yes. And no. I don't know why I picked that movie when you asked. I watched it as a child with my grandmother, and I don't recall much of the plot. I just remember falling in love with the idyllic setting. It made me want to visit New York."

"You've been to New York?" His dark eyes brightened. "That's one of my favorite cities."

Sadie inwardly cringed. Why did she keep saying the wrong thing? She must look like a total lunatic.

"Well, no. I haven't," she admitted, praying for a secret escape hatch to appear in the floorboards. "Not yet. But I plan to. One day. I've been working here full-time since I graduated high school. I don't have much time to travel."

"I see." His features momentarily softened with sympathy, then he smiled again. "So, seeing it on an enormous screen will be the next best thing. Are you free tomorrow night? Say, around seven?"

"Y-yes?" she said, more as a question than a statement.

What was wrong with her? She never got tongue-tied.

"Great. See you then."

He set the letter on the counter beside the valentine before strolling out of the kitchen.

Sadie stared at the piece of paper that held answers to a mystery she'd been dying to solve but couldn't bring herself to care at the moment.

All she could think about was tomorrow night.

Her and Landon. Alone. Watching a movie. In the dark.

Why did that prospect terrify her so much?

CHAPTER 12

Landon stepped out of Sadie's Sweet Shop, welcoming the rush of cold air. He needed the icy blast to slap some sense into him. The idea of a movie night with Sadie was a little too appealing.

Over the last several days, his long-held beliefs about romance and relationships had started to slip, leaving him conflicted in more ways than one.

"Hey!" Ben Carter called from the center of the town square, derailing his thoughts. "Come play catch with us!" The young boy waved his mitt, nearly missing the ball Grant launched in his direction.

Landon's heart warmed. He'd never taken an interest in kids until he met Grant's son. Ben had the kind of affable, sweet-tempered spirit a person couldn't help but love.

He crossed the field, bending to pet their scruffy terrier, Vinny, who seemed to be having the time of his life rolling in a pile of mulch. He grinned, thinking of Reginald, who wouldn't be caught dead anywhere near a mound of decaying leaves.

Once he'd said hello to the adorable mutt, he joined Grant and flipped up the collar of his jacket. "Aren't you guys cold out here?"

"Not really. The exercise keeps your blood flowing. Give it a whirl." Grant tossed him the ball.

With stiff, frozen fingers, Landon gripped the soft leather and lobbed a high pitch toward Ben, who shuffled backward and caught it above his head.

"Great catch!" Landon praised the boy, who gleefully chucked it back to his dad, completing the triangle.

"Trying to show me up with your professional pitches?" Grant teased. "I heard you went to spring training with the Giants a few years ago. That must have been an incredible experience."

"Yeah, it was fun." While Landon had fond memories of the week he'd spent practicing with the team, and was grateful for the opportunity, as he watched Grant with his son, he wondered if there were other more important life experiences he was missing out on.

Before meeting Grant, he'd scoffed at the idea of marriage and family. Growing up, he and his parents had been an inseparable team, enjoying the kind of comfortable camaraderie most people envied. Even as an adult, they'd remained close. But when his dad deserted them when they needed him most, his idealistic view had shattered, along with his mother's heart.

If his devoted and loving family could crumble so easily, what chance did anyone else have of making theirs last?

As if on cue, Eliza emerged from The Calendar Café with a thermos and plate of cookies. "Time to warm up your hands," she called out with her usual robust cheerfulness.

Ben wriggled out of his glove and raced over to join her on

the bench.

Grant laughed. "I'm not sure which Ben enjoys more, playing catch with me or Eliza's snack breaks."

Landon smiled, watching mother and son sit side by side while Eliza filled the thermos cap with a steaming beverage.

They looked so much alike with their fair blond hair and huge, dark eyes. And in retrospect, it didn't surprise Landon that Grant didn't immediately suspect Ben was his son when they first met a couple of years ago. With his dark curls and lavender-blue eyes, Grant didn't look anything like his son, except that they now both wore the same pair of black-rimmed glasses.

After discovering they had a son several years after the fact, a lot of men would've walked away, not wanting to upend their entire lives. But not Grant. He'd taken on fatherhood wholeheartedly, and he'd flourished in the role.

"Do you ever have any regrets?" The question left Landon's lips before the thought had fully formed in his mind.

"About what?"

"The way things turned out over the last few years."

Before becoming a family man, Grant had been on the social fast track in San Francisco. His web design business had taken off, he'd gained notoriety in all the right circles, and his success seemed limitless. What some men worked their whole lives to achieve, Grant had given up in an instant.

"Honestly?" Grant's gaze softened, remaining fixed on his family. "My only regret is not marrying Eliza sooner."

"You dated for almost a year before tying the knot, right?"

"Yeah. At the time, we thought taking it slow would be good for Ben. You know, not introduce too many major changes at once. But looking back, I think he just wanted us to be a family. Which is what I wanted, too. Waiting was one of the hardest things I've ever done." His expression sobered. "It's cliché, but time isn't guaranteed. When you know something's right, why waste it?"

Landon let Grant's question sink in, but it only sparked one of his own.

One he was too reluctant to ask....

How did you know when something was right?

The following night, Sadie sat in her delivery truck, parked outside Landon's home. She smoothed the letter he'd translated against the steering wheel, rereading it one more time, letting Abélard's haunting plea seep into her bones.

Come back to me, my love.

The world has lost all color without you.

Although she'd never experienced that kind of all-consuming affection in the romantic sense, she could relate to a similar kind of emotional desolation; the way the entire world faded to gray when you lost someone you loved.

When faced with the heartache of intense loss, you could no longer taste, smell, or feel anything around you. And everything you once held dear suddenly lacked all meaning and significance. Nothing mattered anymore. Your entire being went numb, to the point you wondered if you'd ever regain any sense of normalcy.

Yes, that unbearable state of existence she knew all too well. And she never wanted to go through it again.

She folded the letter and slipped it into the glove box before climbing out of the driver's seat, silently reciting her mental monologue for the evening.

So, Landon, since I'm here, I thought we could discuss our plans for the booth and finally come to a resolution. If we're each willing to compromise, I think we can come to a satisfactory solution for both of us....

As the words played on repeat in her mind, she gained some confidence in her step.

Discussing the festival during the movie would be the perfect strategy to prevent the evening from feeling too much like a date. Plus, it would keep her thoughts from drifting to places they had no business going... like summoning visions of Landon's arm around her on an all-too-cozy couch.

Riddled with nerves again, Sadie rang the doorbell and eagerly anticipated Gladys's warm, welcoming smile, hoping it would put her at ease.

But when the door finally opened, her heartbeat faltered.

Landon smiled at her from across the threshold. "Hi."

Something about his soft, intimate tone sent ripples down her spine. Not to mention he looked almost huggable in a hunter-green cashmere sweater paired with dark denim jeans. He managed to pull off both casual and catalog-worthy.

She tossed her ponytail over her shoulder and swept aside a few flyaways with her gloved finger, chiding herself for suddenly caring about her appearance. "Where's Gladys?"

"She has the night off." He stepped to the side, and as she brushed past him, she tried not to notice the delicious spicy citrus scent of his cologne that reminded her of orange and cardamom truffles.

"Will your mother be joining us for the movie?" she asked hopefully as she followed him down a long corridor.

"I invited her, but she's deep into a Mary Higgins Clark novel and needs to know the ending."

"That's a shame." She tried to keep her voice even and not give away how desperate she was not to be alone with him.

She searched her mind for the speech she'd planned about the booth, but all cognitive abilities vanished the second she stepped inside the spacious home theater.

Miraculously, Landon had transformed the entire room into a mini New York City. Cardboard cutouts of the towering skyline flanked both sides of the colossal screen, each tiny window lit up by twinkling lights. A savory, mouth-watering aroma wafted from several rolling snack carts made to resemble street vendors offering New York specialties like falafel and fresh bagels.

Her shocked gaze took in the neon signs denoting famous locales, like Broadway and Times Square, before finally landing on Landon's face. "Does it always look like this?"

A hopelessly foolish part of her wanted to believe he'd done it for her, but why would he go through all that trouble for someone he barely even liked?

He shifted his weight, one hand stuffed inside his front pocket, appearing uncharacteristically self-conscious. "No. I just thought it would be fun for our movie night."

Sadie continued to stare, unable to string two words together as her heart pounded inside her chest. She had no idea what to make of this man.

He cleared his throat. "Are you hungry?"

"Starving, actually," she admitted, anxious for a distraction. "And it smells amazing."

While they loaded up their plates, Sadie noticed the labels on some of the boxes. As if he hadn't already gone out of his way to make the evening special, he'd had half the food delivered all the way from New York! She couldn't believe it.

Her stomach fluttered as she followed him to the front

row where, instead of separate recliners, he settled onto a buttery soft couch with plenty of room for two. She recalled the mental image from earlier, and a blush crept across her cheeks. Luckily, he didn't appear to notice.

He pushed a button on the side and folding tables popped open on either end. Landon set his plate on one and gestured toward its twin.

Sadie followed his lead before sitting beside him, acutely aware of their close proximity.

"Blanket?" He offered her a velvety throw, which she gladly accepted, if only to provide a subtle barrier between them.

As the movie started and idyllic snapshots of autumn in New York scrolled across the enormous screen, Sadie's nerves began to settle.

She forgot all about her plan to discuss the booth and allowed herself to be transported to the spellbinding city, made even more magical by Landon's thoughtful additions.

When they'd finished their food, Sadie snuggled deeper into the blanket, still able to feel the heat from Landon's body radiate through the plush fabric.

Although it made no sense, being so close to him felt at once comfortable and exhilarating. The tension in her muscles relaxed, but her skin tingled, and she found it inordinately difficult to concentrate on the movie. But as the plot unfolded, she quickly realized she'd be better off if she didn't.

To her horror, she'd inadvertently chosen a film that all too closely resembled her situation with Landon—a small bookshop owner battling the CEO of a big-box store about to put her out of business.

Her cheeks burned at the similarities.

Would Landon notice them, too?

CHAPTER 13

When Sadie first picked *You've Got Mail,* Landon didn't give any thought to whether or not he'd enjoy the movie. In all honesty, it didn't really matter. He just wanted to spend time with her. They could sit through a three-hour documentary on watching bread rise, for all he cared.

But as the film progressed, and the plot registered, he found himself keenly interested in how things between the main couple would play out. And yet, he wasn't prepared for the emotional mix of triumph and satisfaction he felt as the closing scene approached, promising a long-awaited happily ever after.

As a symphonic, sentimental rendition of "Over the Rainbow" floated from the speakers, the awareness of Sadie's presence beside him magnified tenfold. He heard every intake of breath and sensed every miniscule movement.

His pulse spiked, beating an audible rhythm in his eardrums—one he hoped Sadie couldn't hear as well. Meg Ryan locked eyes with Tom Hanks on screen, tearfully watching him walk toward her, and Landon couldn't help stealing a glance at Sadie.

He could trace the outline of her profile in the soft glow but couldn't read her expression. He'd give anything to know what she was thinking at that moment.

The Hollywood couple kissed, and with the swell of a crescendo, the camera panned to the clouds as though granting them privacy.

Landon didn't dare move as the room darkened with the closing credits and the melodic vocals of Carole King crooning "Anyone at All" serenaded them in the stillness.

Sadie shifted beside him, and he stole another glance. A silky strand of hair had escaped her ponytail and fell across her forehead, silently tempting him.

Driven by an overpowering impulse that overrode all reason, he swept it aside.

A spark of awareness rippled up his arm, blazing across his skin like a sudden exchange of thermal energy.

At the startling and spontaneous contact, her gaze flickered to meet his in the darkness, her eyes wide and questioning.

He wasn't sure what made him do it—the music, perhaps, or the overflow of emotions from the film—but either way, he seemed to be outside of himself. His heart beating wildly, he leaned forward, once again reaching out his hand.

This time, his fingertips grazed her cheekbone, tracing the delicate contour of her face.

She shivered but didn't pull away.

His gaze fell to her lips, perfect and slightly parted.

Was he really going to do this? If he did, it would change everything.

Don't think. Don't waste time.

He gently lifted her chin, but as unexpectedly as she'd leaned into him, she suddenly stiffened.

In one jerky, gut-wrenching movement, she shifted away from him—the moment lost. For several seconds, Landon sat motionless, unsure how to repair the situation… and his pride.

How could he have been so foolish to think Sadie would reciprocate his feelings? Feelings he didn't even understand himself.

But then, for a brief instant, it had seemed possible.

Where had he gone wrong?

He steadied his uneven breath and asked, "So, what did you think of the movie? Just like you remembered it?" Not the smoothest segue, but he didn't know what else to say.

"Not really." Her response seemed to be a silent agreement to pretend like nothing had happened between them. For which he was grateful. "Actually," she continued, "I found it incredibly unrealistic."

"How so?"

"They never would've fallen in love in real life."

She sounded so certain, he couldn't help asking, "What makes you say that?"

By now, the closing credits score had switched to an upbeat rendition of "I'm Gonna Sit Right Down and Write Myself a Letter." The happy, carefree vocals of Billy Williams added to the awkward tension.

Sadie kept her gaze fixed straight ahead. "He ruined her business. That's not something a girl forgets. Or forgives."

Landon blinked, surprised by the intensity of her tone. Was that really her takeaway from the film? "To be fair, her business was already failing." He immediately knew he'd said the wrong thing because her spine went rigid.

"Yes, but she could have saved it. Although, we'll never know, will we? Because once he opened his humongous bookstore with its fancy coffee shop and endless amenities, she didn't stand a chance."

"Maybe..." he said slowly, trying to understand her negative viewpoint. That wasn't how he'd seen the situation at all. "But what about her new job at the end? Don't you think she was happy with how it all turned out?"

"She made the best of circumstances that were beyond her control. But how happy could she be? She'd lost the business her grandmother built from nothing."

"Her mother," he kindly corrected.

"What?"

"You said her *grandmother*. But it was her mother's bookstore, remember?"

"Oh, right," she said quickly, seeming flustered. "Well, either way. She lost more than a bookshop. She lost a legacy. And in real life, there's no way she would have forgiven him for that."

As her words sank in, Landon wondered if maybe they weren't talking about the movie after all.

~

Sadie sat in the driveway, staring at the soft glow behind their living room curtains.

Gigi had waited up for her, no doubt anticipating a complete rundown of the night's events. But what could she say? Her hands still shook whenever she thought about Landon's fingertips against her skin and the intense, tender look in his dark eyes as he'd leaned down to—

Dismissing the memory, she bit her lower lip, unwilling to

let her mind wander back to that moment. Every time she relived the almost-kiss, her head spun, her thoughts a dizzying whirl of desire and fear.

She'd never wanted romance or the risky entanglement of falling in love. Attachments of any kind led to heartache, and she had enough people in her life to worry about. The constant weight of concern that something catastrophic could happen any second never left her shoulders.

Not to mention, falling for Landon would be a betrayal of her grandmother's life's work and everything they stood for, both professionally and personally.

Her phone buzzed in her purse, and as she withdrew it, Lucy's contact photo appeared on screen, her bright, buoyant smile in stark contrast with Sadie's melancholy mood.

Sadie let the call go to voice mail, knowing she wouldn't be able to fend off her friend's dogged pursuit of all the evening's minute details. And armed with the kind of ammunition afforded by their almost-kiss, her relentless setup attempts would become even more unbearable.

Sometimes, Sadie wondered if Lucy's persistent matchmaking stemmed from guilt. They used to joke about growing old together, living in the same house, and getting into all sorts of shenanigans like the Golden Girls. But a few months ago, Lucy had fallen hard for Vick Johnson, a former marine who'd worked for her brother at the diner and helped out around Bill Tucker's farm. They'd even adopted a precious yellow Lab puppy together and quickly became a cozy little family.

Ever since, Lucy had been determined for Sadie to find someone, too, despite her unwavering insistence that she wanted to remain single.

As she slid the phone back inside her purse, Sadie paused when a text from Lucy pinged on the screen.

Emergency. Call me ASAP.

The second she read the ominous words, her heart plummeted into her stomach.

She immediately returned Lucy's call, forgoing the pleasantries. "What's wrong?"

"We need help, and I don't know what to do," Lucy blurted, her tone high-pitched and strained with worry. "Peggy Sue went into early labor, and Bill isn't home. We left him a voice mail, but don't know if he'll get it in time."

A wave of relief followed by renewed panic surged through Sadie. While she was glad Lucy and Vick weren't the ones in trouble, everyone in town knew the pet pig was Bill's pride and joy, especially since the death of his wife, who'd raised Peggy Sue from birth. If anything happened to her during labor, or to any of her piglets, the gentle-hearted farmer would be devastated.

"Did you call a vet?"

"Yes, but the nearest one is in Primrose Valley and already out on an emergency call. Everyone else is too far away and wouldn't get here in time." Lucy's voice warbled as she fought back tears. "Sadie, I don't know if we can do this. We've tried to make the barn warm and comfortable, and Vick looked up how-to videos online, but what if something goes wrong?"

Sadie jerked on her seat belt, clicking it into place. "Just do what you can. I'll be there as soon as possible."

"You know about farrowing?" Lucy asked in surprise.

"No, but I know someone who does."

If only she could convince her to help.

CHAPTER 14

Sitting in the darkness of the den, Landon gazed into the flickering firelight, mulling over how the evening had gone horribly wrong... *again*.

He couldn't seem to spend one night around Sadie without putting his foot in his mouth. Even when his sole intent was to guarantee she had a good time, he inadvertently said something to upset her. Was the unfortunate pattern doomed to repeat itself?

Car headlights streamed through the front window, disrupting his thoughts. Who would be coming by at this time of night?

He rose from the couch and peered outside, stunned to see Sadie's delivery truck stop in the driveway. Had she left something behind?

His stomach flip-flopped, a jumble of anxious anticipation.

Play it cool, man.

He forced his legs to take slow, steady strides to greet her at the front door, despite his eagerness.

"Miss me already?" He smiled, hoping his greeting came

off as lighthearted teasing and not too forward. Although, as he asked the playful question, he realized something startling —*he'd* missed *her*.

"I'm actually here to see your mother, if it's not too late." She twisted her hands, the nervous flicker in her eyes betraying her hesitation.

"Is everything okay?" He moved aside to let her enter, shutting the door to the cold night air.

"Not really. But it's a long story. Is your mother still awake?"

"Most likely. She's probably in the library." He led the way, his pulse pumping wildly, wondering what could be wrong. And how he could help.

Irene glanced up from her late-night reading when she heard them approach. "Sadie! What a nice surprise. Is the movie just now ending? I must've lost track of time." She closed the book, keeping one finger tucked in the spine. "It's so nice of you to come say goodbye before you head home."

"Actually"—Sadie shifted her feet—"I came to ask a favor."

"Oh? What can I do?"

They both listened intently as Sadie explained the situation at Bill Tucker's farm, trying to keep her tone calm and even. But despite her best efforts, Landon noticed the slight tremor in her voice and the way her muscles tensed with a sense of earnestness and desperation.

He immediately wanted to fix things for her, to assure her it would all be okay. But what could he do? His gaze darted to his mother, who held the answer to the problem. But would she help? He wasn't so sure.

"I realize I'm asking a lot." Some of the urgency vanished from Sadie's voice, replaced by a softness that revealed compassion and understanding. "And I feel terrible for putting you in this position. Especially at the last minute. But we really need you. Please say you'll come."

Irene slipped her finger from between the pages, her novel forgotten. "I—I don't think I can. I don't have my practice anymore."

"But you remember how?" Sadie asked.

"I suppose," Irene said slowly. "But I haven't worked with animals since..." She glanced at her wheelchair, her features strained.

"Irene..." Sadie took a step forward. The tension slipped from her shoulders, as though releasing all intent or pretext. She even seemed to forget he was with them in the room. When she spoke, she held Irene's gaze with an openness and vulnerability. "I can't pretend to know what you've gone through or why you quit your practice or why you don't like to leave this house. And if you say no, I'll understand. It's entirely your decision. But while we may not know each other very well, in my heart of hearts, I believe you have all the skill in the world. And there's no one I'd trust more to help deliver these piglets safely."

Landon's chest tightened as something flashed in his mother's eyes, something he hadn't seen in years—a glimmer of hope and purpose.

She lifted her chin a little higher as she said, "I'll need my medical bag from the back of my closet."

Sadie clasped both hands together in gratitude. "Thank you, thank you!"

Landon released the breath he'd been holding, shocked and elated his mother had agreed to help.

As he volunteered to gather the supplies she needed, he said a silent prayer everything would go smoothly, without so much as a hiccup.

He wasn't sure his mom's fragile mental state could survive anything less.

~

Landon marveled as his mother entered the barn with all the poise and confidence he remembered from his youth. She'd been a regular Dr. Dolittle during his childhood, working miracles with animals other vets deemed beyond hope.

Then, one day, everything changed.

Landon shook away the thought, focusing on the present.

Vick and Lucy had created a cozy nest for Peggy Sue with straw and blankets, and strategically placed heat lamps to dispel the harsh winter chill.

They'd both rejoiced at their arrival, grateful for Irene's skill and expertise, and their appreciation and faith in her abilities seemed to buoy his mother's spirits even more.

"Landon." She caught his attention with her crisp, commanding tone. "I'll need you to keep track of the time between piglets. Let me know if we start to go past forty minutes."

"On it." Landon tapped his watch, and, as if on cue, Peggy Sue grunted and squealed, sending everyone scurrying to their assigned posts, ready to assist when needed.

For the most part, the stalwart sow knew exactly what to do, and her adorable—albeit slimy—offspring made their way into the world in smooth, regular intervals of fifteen to twenty minutes.

Landon had never witnessed a live birth before and stood in awe of Peggy Sue's strength and endurance.

From her wheelchair, Irene gave instructions to Vick on

how to check each piglet and cut the umbilical cord, while Lucy and Sadie gave them a quick cleaning before sending them back to Peggy Sue to nurse.

Landon continued to keep the time, watching his mother work with unabashed pride. He hadn't seen her this alive and vibrant in years, and he owed it all to Sadie.

He stole a glance in her direction, and their eyes locked.

She cradled the tiniest polka-dotted piglet in her arms, her eyes shining as she smiled up at him. In that moment, all their differences and underlying conflict vanished in light of the miracle before them, and the intimacy of the shared glance momentarily stole his breath.

Her gaze flickered to Irene and her smile deepened, as if she, too, understood tonight's significance.

Somehow, encapsulated in the warmth and soft glow of the farrowing barn, time seemed to slow down, and he could finally see things clearly.

He was falling for Sadie Hamilton.

And he didn't care if it made sense.

"Landon, how long has it been since the last piglet?" His mother's tense voice broke through his reverie, jerking the world back into focus.

He checked his watch, and his heart sank. "Forty-six minutes."

"That's too long. She's going to need our help with the next one."

"What can I do?" Vick knelt by Peggy Sue's side, ready to jump into action, but Irene shook her head.

"We'll need to pull the piglet out, and your hands are too big."

Landon's chest cinched at the uncertain waver in his mother's voice.

Please, please don't let us lose one of the piglets, he silently prayed, his fears on the verge of coming to fruition.

"I can help," Sadie offered, though her apprehension was evident.

Landon admired her willingness, and hoped his mother would at least let her try, instead of giving up altogether.

To his surprise, she straightened and turned to face him. "Set me behind Peggy Sue, then hand me my gloves and the lubricant from my medical bag."

Had he heard her correctly? Was she really going to deliver the piglet on her own?

"Landon?" she repeated, louder this time.

He snapped to attention and did as she requested, being careful to keep her lower body wrapped in the blanket as he eased her onto the bed of hay, all the while continuing to pray.

For the next few minutes, they waited with bated breath, the hum of the space heaters and Peggy Sue's heavy breathing filling the silence.

Tension sizzled through the air.

"I got your message. How is she—" Bill Tucker burst into the barn, his towering frame casting a shadow across the straw-covered floor. His voice fell away as his gaze landed on Irene and Peggy Sue. Instantly sobered, he removed his cowboy hat and pressed it against his chest, his rugged features etched with worry.

"She's doing just fine." Vick clasped his broad shoulder with a reassuring squeeze. "Irene is a vet."

Bill nodded in silent understanding, his eyes trained on Irene, observing her every move with all the paternal anxiety of a father waiting for his first child to be born.

The entire barn went still as Irene slowly withdrew her hand.

Sadie fought back tears as a perfect pink piglet emerged into the world, safe and sound.

Exhausted after successfully delivering eleven beautiful babies, Peggy Sue collapsed with a dramatic sigh, and Bill rushed to her side, his face awash with relief.

"Good job, mama." Irene set the runt of the litter with its brothers and sisters to nurse. "You did great."

"I don't know how to thank you." His tone husky, Bill gazed at Irene as though she'd just descended from the heavens.

Sadie thought she noticed the faintest blush dapple Irene's cheeks, but it was difficult to tell in the dim light of the barn.

"A thank-you isn't necessary. I'm happy I could help."

"Please visit the piglets any time you want," Bill told her, stroking the top of Peggy Sue's head.

"I'd like that."

This time, Irene's blush was unmistakable, and it took all of Sadie's self-control not to grin like a giddy schoolgirl. Did she detect a mini crush forming between Bill and Irene?

She cast a glance at Landon, who looked flummoxed by the exchange, although he must be pleased his mother had agreed to leave the house again.

"Would you like help getting back into your chair?" Vick asked kindly.

Although well intentioned, his question snuffed the light from Irene's eyes, and she immediately averted her gaze, shrinking into herself.

"I've got it." Landon stepped forward and carefully scooped his mother into his arms.

While he returned her to the chair, Irene kept her chin

tucked inward, shielding her face from Bill with a veil of her dark hair.

Sadie's heart twisted with sympathy, although she didn't think Irene had anything to be embarrassed about.

"That's a nice model." Bill gestured toward the motorized chair with his wide-brimmed hat. "My wife's didn't have all those bells and whistles."

Surprised, Irene lifted her head. "Your wife used a wheelchair?"

"Yes, ma'am. For the last few years before she passed. But it wasn't anythin' fancy. Although, we had fun with it. We used to race. Her in the chair and me on the riding lawn mower."

This sparked a smile from Irene.

Sadie could've hugged Bill right then and there for putting Irene at ease. Maybe the giant, soft-spoken farmer would be the man to draw her out of her shell.

One of the piglets squealed, disrupting the moment, and all eyes turned to the little butterball as it struggled to free its hoof from Irene's afghan.

The next few minutes seemed to unfold in slow motion as Irene scrambled to untangle the little tike, to no avail.

All the color drained from her face as the blanket slipped from her lap, revealing what she'd desperately tried to keep hidden.

CHAPTER 15

For a moment, Landon couldn't move.

A familiar hardness settled in his stomach. The painful kind. The kind that meant he knew exactly what would happen next, but he couldn't do anything to stop it.

Her features ashen, his mother yanked the blanket back over her lap, concealing the evidence of her missing leg.

Not that it mattered. Everyone had already noticed. Of course, that didn't matter, either.

He'd tried to convince her that no one—especially not anyone in Poppy Creek—would view her any differently, but she wouldn't listen. She'd gotten it into her head that it made her less of a person. Less worthy. Less valuable. Less… whole.

And it ate him up inside.

"It's time to go home," she murmured, barely above a whisper.

"Irene—" Sadie stepped forward, but his mother acted as though she hadn't heard her and rolled toward the open door, slipping into the darkness before anyone else could protest.

Landon turned toward Sadie and ran a hand through his

hair, struggling for something to say, a way to explain, to apologize.

"Go," she said gently. "I'll get a ride back to my truck later."

Even though he hated for the night to end like this, he offered a grateful nod. Somehow, she understood that they'd needed time alone without him having to ask.

Torn, he turned toward Bill, Lucy, and Vick. Although he opened his mouth to speak, no words came out. What could he say in a situation like this?

"Thanks for everything you've done tonight, son," Bill said graciously, tipping his hat. "You and your mother. Peggy Sue and I are indebted to you both."

"You're welcome." The words scratched his throat, and Landon cleared it, surprised by the emotions rising to the surface.

These people were kind and caring, exactly the sort of folks his mother needed in her life, yet he'd be surprised if she ever gave them—or herself—another chance.

"Good night." With the lackluster goodbye, he retreated outside into the biting cold.

His mother waited for him beside the van and didn't utter a word as he helped her get situated and shut the door. Her silence continued as they rattled down the dirt road toward home.

The ink-black night consumed them, matching the bleak mood weighing down the air inside the van until it became difficult to breathe.

Landon glanced in the rearview mirror.

His mother sat hunched over, barely recognizable from the woman she'd been hours earlier. Her hands, which had just brought a piglet safely into the world with care and precision, now lay coiled in her lap, occasionally picking at a thread on the afghan. The afghan she used as a shield. The afghan that had betrayed her biggest insecurity.

Landon's fingers ached, and he realized he'd been clenching the steering wheel so tightly, he could see the veins on the backs of his hands. He loosened his grip, focusing on taking deep, even breaths.

In times like these, it was easiest to blame his father.

Landon's throat constricted, and he blinked several times. He wanted to close his eyes, to block out the memories, but he kept his gaze fixed on the beams of light illuminating the road ahead.

The day he'd received the call from the hospital, all his illusions of a secure, happy family had been destroyed in a single moment. He'd known his parents had struggles, especially around his mother's illness, but he hadn't been prepared for that phone call… or what came after.

He hadn't even known his mother needed surgery to remove her leg until the hospital called after the procedure, which had also come as a surprise, since his dad was her emergency contact.

A few minutes after he'd hung up the phone—shocked and confused—his dad texted. Seven simple words that completely changed his life.

I'm sorry. I can't do this anymore.

Landon could still see the cowardly cop-out as though it had been burned into his brain. Was it any wonder his mother believed people would abandon her just like his father had?

His eyes stung, and he struggled to keep his composure as they pulled into the driveway, and he helped her inside.

In the hallway, before they parted ways for the night, he bent down and wrapped his arms around her.

She remained limp in his embrace, but he only hugged her tighter.

"I love you, Mom."

For a fraction of a second, she leaned her head against his shoulder.

As he held her, he noticed how small she felt, how vulnerable.

And he renewed his resolve to do whatever it took to take care of her.

Even if it meant making more sacrifices of his own.

Sitting cross-legged on the soft straw, Sadie leaned against a bale of hay beside Lucy, watching the piglets sleep.

Everything about the scene should have evoked contentment and tranquility. The adorable vignette of mother and babies snuggled together in their cozy nest. The gentle hum of the space heaters. The flickering light of the lanterns. Even the novelty of a pseudo slumber party with Lucy in order to keep an eye on the piglets during their first night should have made her happy. But she couldn't stop thinking about Irene.

Every time she replayed the look on Irene's face when the afghan fell away, her heart ached.

Lucy shifted onto her other side and pulled the wool blanket tighter around herself. "Thinking about Irene?"

"Yeah," Sadie whispered, her throat raw with emotion.

"Me, too. I wish I'd known what to say. I feel awful that she left like that, worried we were judging her."

"I know. I thought the same thing." Sadie leaned her head back but didn't close her eyes. Because if she did, she'd see the haunted look on Landon's face, too, and she couldn't handle that.

"How do you tell someone that something like that doesn't matter without minimizing what they've been through?" Lucy mused. "I can't pretend to know what it feels like, but it also doesn't make me think any less of her."

"Me, either. In fact, the more time I spend with her, the more amazing I think she is."

"From what I saw, Bill thinks she's pretty amazing, too." A sly smile broke through Lucy's somber expression, and Sadie couldn't help reciprocating.

"There was definitely some chemistry there."

"I haven't seen Bill interested in anyone since his wife passed away over ten years ago. And Irene seemed to like him, too." Lucy picked a piece of straw out of her hair and twisted it between her fingers. "Do you know what happened to Landon's dad?"

"I don't," Sadie admitted. There was a lot she didn't know about Landon, and to her surprise, she wanted that to change.

"Well, I think it's time Irene came out of hiding and got an honest-to-goodness Poppy Creek welcome. It's a shame more folks haven't met her."

"I agree, but I don't know how we're going to make that happen. She can be stubborn."

"So can you." Lucy grinned, and Sadie scooped a handful of soft wood shavings and tossed them at her playfully.

Lucy laughed, swatting them away.

"Okay, you have a point," Sadie conceded. "I'll think of something."

"Maybe Landon has a few ideas? You should ask him." Lucy's blue eyes twinkled in the soft glow of the space heaters.

For the first time, Sadie didn't instinctively revolt at her friend's not-so-subtle hint, as though her heart was softening to the possibility.

She immediately pushed the thought aside.

This wasn't about Landon. Or her and Landon.

It was about Irene.

And an idea suddenly popped into her head that just might work.

CHAPTER 16

"Miss Sadie, how nice to see you!" Gladys greeted her with a glowing smile. "I'm afraid Mr. Landon isn't home today."

"No problem. I'm actually here to see Irene."

"Oh." Gladys's smile faltered, but she quickly recovered. "Come in, come in. I'll have you wait in the den while I find her."

Sadie didn't mind waiting, but she suspected *while I find her* was really code for *while I find out if she'll agree to see you.*

Sure enough, a few minutes later, Gladys returned, and from the look on her face, she wasn't bearing good news. "Apologies, but Miss Irene isn't feeling up to having visitors right now."

"That's okay." Sadie plucked a *Popular Science* magazine off the coffee table and sank deeper into the couch. "I'll wait."

Gladys's eyebrows lifted in surprise, but Sadie wasn't going to give up that easily. "Please let her know I'll be waiting here for as long as it takes."

"Certainly, dear." The older woman turned slowly and

shuffled out of the room as though she didn't quite know what to make of the situation.

Sadie absentmindedly flipped through the pages of the magazine while the minutes turned into nearly an hour with no sign of Gladys or Irene. She glanced at the grandfather clock.

Based on their agreed upon buffer of time, Gigi would be here any moment for phase one of the plan: bring Truffle or BonBon to Irene for an "emergency" checkup, then casually mention how they're in desperate need of a veterinarian in Poppy Creek. Sadie hoped to use Gigi's charm to plant the subtle hint that Irene was exactly what the town needed.

Of course, the strategy would never work if Irene wouldn't even agree to see them. Sadie had given herself the job of drawing Irene out of hiding, then she'd introduce Gigi. But so far, it looked like she'd failed.

Just then, the whir of Irene's wheelchair interrupted her thoughts.

"You're still here?" Irene rolled to a stop in front of the fireplace.

Reginald snuggled in her lap and eyed Sadie with open suspicion.

Sadie set down the magazine. "Yep. And I'm not going anywhere."

She meant in more general terms, even beyond that afternoon, and based on the way Irene's features softened, she hadn't missed the subtext.

"Actually, there's someone I'd like you to meet," Sadie continued, and with perfect timing, car tires crunched across the gravel drive, signaling Gigi's arrival.

Excited for their plan to unfold, Sadie ambled to the

window and peered between the curtains. Gigi climbed out of her red Cadillac clad in a fluffy faux fur coat and hat à la *Doctor Zhivago,* and BonBon and Truffle bounded out after her, their bushy tails swishing in eager anticipation. It wasn't every day they went on a special outing, and they both wore large, frilly bows around their collars to celebrate the occasion.

Sadie shook her head in amusement. Of course Gigi would bend the rules and bring both cats instead of one. She had a habit of going overboard.

As Sadie turned away from the window, she heard another set of tires and whirled back around. Lucy's gold Mercedes rolled to a stop beside Gigi's Cadillac.

Sadie frowned in confusion as her friend emerged from the driver's seat cradling her chubby yellow Labrador, Tink.

What were they doing here?

The rambunctious pup wriggled free from Lucy's arms and plodded after BonBon and Truffle, who politely tolerated her presence, though they didn't appear pleased. Especially since Tink persisted in batting their oversize bows with her pudgy paw.

Sadie bit back a groan. Although she adored Lucy and Tink, the pup was barely housebroken. And the whole scheme relied on subtlety. What was Gigi thinking inviting Lucy to come along? As she tried to manufacture a plausible excuse for their presence to Irene, more crunching gravel drew her attention.

Horrified, Sadie gaped as a veritable circus unloaded in the driveway.

Penny Davis with her Russian tortoise, Chip. Kat Bennett with her snow-white husky mix, Fitz. Olivia with Reed's cockatiel, Nips. Eliza and her wiry gray terrier, Vinny. Even

Cassie came along, acting as a chauffeur for Dolores Whittaker and her portly tabby cat, Banjo.

Apparently, Gigi had taken it upon herself to include half the town in their scheme. Frantic, Sadie yanked the curtains closed.

"What's going on?" Irene asked.

"N-nothing. I mean, nothing I can't handle," Sadie stammered. She needed to do something before Gigi escorted the entire zoo into Irene's home.

The doorbell rang, and Sadie nearly jumped out of her skin.

"You seem nervous." Irene's eyes narrowed. "Who is it that you want me to meet?"

"I'll explain in a second, but first I need to take care of something." Sadie dashed toward the double doors, intent on stopping the bizarre parade of pets before they ruined everything, but she wasn't quick enough.

Gladys entered, her eyes wide in bewilderment. "Miss Irene, you have a few more visitors."

Sadie froze, unable to move as Gigi swept into the room, followed by her eclectic entourage. Shock flickered across Irene's now-pale features, but before Sadie had a chance to explain—or at least, to *try* to explain—Gigi stepped forward with a flourish.

"Irene, it's a pleasure to finally meet you. I'm Gigi, Sadie's grandmother. I've heard such wonderful things about you."

"You have?" Irene's uneasy gaze darted to Sadie, who looked on helplessly.

"Of course!" Gigi beamed. "Sadie adores you. And after we all heard what you did for sweet Bill Tucker and Peggy Sue last night, we couldn't believe our good fortune."

"I—I don't understand." Irene nervously smoothed the

afghan across her lap, looking about as uncomfortable as Sadie felt.

"Oh, it's quite simple, chérie." Gigi's smile didn't waver for a second. "It's about time Poppy Creek had its own veterinarian. And we think you'd be a perfect fit."

"But... you don't even know me." Irene gazed at Gigi as though she'd lost her mind.

"We know everything we need to know. You're a skilled vet with a passion and love for animals," Gigi said matter-of-factly. "Besides, if my granddaughter likes you, that's good enough for me."

"That's very kind, but—"

"No buts," Gigi interrupted. "Look at these precious faces and tell me you don't want to be their vet."

The cutest of the bunch, chunky—and adorably uncoordinated—Tink stumbled forward on her plump little legs to plead their case. She apparently misunderstood her assignment because she squatted in the middle of the priceless Persian rug and proudly peed as though she were giving an encore performance.

A collective gasp rippled through the room, and Lucy sprang forward, plucking her offending pup off the floor. "I'm so, *so* sorry. We've been potty training her, and she hasn't had an accident in days. Whatever it takes, I promise to clean your carpet until it's as good as new."

Mortified, Sadie held her breath, waiting for Irene to order them all out of the house and to never come back.

But to her surprise, a tiny snort escaped Irene's lips, followed by a burst of laughter. The kind of wholehearted bubbles-from-the-center-of-your-being laughter that made her shoulders shake and tears stream down her cheeks.

Sadie blinked. Had Irene finally succumbed to the shock and had a nervous breakdown?

Wiping aside her tears, Irene turned to Gladys. "Would you put on a pot of tea, please? I may regret this decision, but I'd like our guests to stay awhile."

~

When Landon arrived home early that evening, entering through the back entrance from his private landing strip, he went straight to the library in search of his mother. With each step, he prayed he'd find her in better spirits than when he'd left. But if he didn't, he had a few ideas to cheer her up.

As he neared the entryway, his gait slowed. Did he hear laughter and voices?

Puzzled, he pushed open the door and froze in his tracks.

At the far end of the room, situated in the conservatory, his mother sat around a long patio table with several women he recognized, chatting over an elaborate tea service.

If that wasn't startling enough, a small pack of dogs played nearby, while Reggie looked on with mild annoyance from his throne-like bed in front of the fire. A well-fed tabby reclined on the mantel above him, and two other felines—much larger than most house cats he'd ever seen—snuggled on the love seat.

Even stranger, a contented cockatiel nibbled on fresh papaya from inside its birdcage on the side table while a large tortoise snoozed underneath.

The unusual scene more closely resembled a bizarre dream than reality, and Landon blinked a few times to make sure he wasn't imagining the whole thing.

His gaze drifted from the odd menagerie back to the animated group of women, zeroing in on Sadie. She smiled when she saw him and silently slipped from the table, dodging the frolicking pups to meet him by the doorway.

With a light hand on his arm, she led him into the hall. Even through the wool fabric of his blazer, her touch made his throat go dry. He coughed, trying to concentrate on anything other than her nearness. "What's going on in there?"

"Something wonderful." Sadie beamed, her eyes shining. "But I wanted to explain before the others saw you."

Landon listened, barely able to believe her story, as Sadie described how half the pets in Poppy Creek had wound up in his library.

"So... you did this?" he asked slowly once she'd finished.

"Not exactly. I had the initial idea, but Gigi is the one who deserves the credit. I thought she'd taken things too far, but it turns out, it was exactly what your mother needed. She's having a great time and is actually considering reopening her veterinary practice."

"You're kidding." Landon's heart surged with hope, but he didn't want to get ahead of himself. It still sounded too good to be true.

"I'm completely serious. She might even join the women's book club."

Landon ran a hand through his hair, struggling to process it all. The very thing he hadn't been able to accomplish in several weeks, Sadie managed to pull off in a matter of days. But would it last?

"What's wrong?" The happy flutter in Sadie's voice faltered. "I thought you'd be pleased."

"I am. I'm just... stunned. I can't believe it."

"Well, believe it." Her grin returned, and it brightened her entire face, momentarily stealing his breath.

Did she have any idea how beautiful she was when she smiled?

And to top it off, she'd performed a miracle, demonstrating her true beauty within. It took all his self-control not to sweep her off the ground in a bear hug.

"I don't know what to say. Except thank you. And if there's any way I can repay the favor, let me know."

"You could tell the world you like chocolate," she teased.

Her playful remark caught him off guard, and it took him a moment to recover. He liked this lighthearted side of her, and that she felt comfortable enough to poke fun, even if it was at his expense.

She must have mistaken his silence for offense because she rushed to add, "I'm just kidding. No favor is necessary. Your mother is incredible, and I'm thrilled she wants to be a part of the community. You can abhor sugar as much as you'd like."

"About that..." He reached into his coat pocket and withdrew the paper heart. The one he'd assumed was Grant's based on the uncanny similarities. The one he'd carried around all day because it felt like keeping a tiny piece of her with him. "I finally opened my valentine."

Her eyes widened in surprise. "But that's—"

"Yours," he finished for her. "Yes, I know. One private candy-making class with Sadie Hamilton."

Her cheeks turned an adorable shade of pink. "Well, this is awkward." She chewed her bottom lip before offering, "You don't have to go through with it. I know it's the last thing you'd ever want to do."

A few days ago, he might have agreed. But standing across

from her now, he'd do almost anything to spend more time with her... even if it involved copious amounts of sugar.

"But isn't that against the rules of the Saint Valentine Swap?"

"There aren't rules, per se. It's more the spirit of the tradition. But I won't tell anyone if you won't."

Landon mulled over her offer, wanting to believe she only gave him a way out for his benefit, not because she loathed the prospect herself. He stuffed the valentine back inside his pocket. "I'm not one to buck tradition. Let me know what evening works for you, and I'll be there."

Her gaze darted to meet his in surprise. "Really? *You're* going to make candy?"

"I can't promise it'll be edible, but I'll do my best."

She continued to stare at him with incredulity. "You're sure it's a good idea?"

"I won't spontaneously combust at the sight of sugar, if that's what you're worried about."

"If you say so." She grinned again.

At the enticing sight, heat shot through him, melting his better judgment while letting in wild thoughts best kept locked in his subconscious.

Such as... What would it be like to kiss her?

Maybe spending time alone wasn't such a brilliant idea after all.

CHAPTER 17

For the first time in her life, Sadie wished the kitchen of the sweet shop had harsh fluorescent lights. The soft white bulbs and homey aroma of cocoa and vanilla felt far too intimate with Landon standing beside her.

"So, what would you like to make?" She looped an apron over her head and readjusted her ponytail.

"What do you suggest?" He followed her lead, donning one of the sweet shop's signature red aprons, somehow making the shapeless garment look sexy.

In truth, she'd gone over several options before he arrived, but she still had a hard time wrapping her mind around the prospect of making candy with Landon Morris.

"How about I go easy on you?" she teased. Keeping his sugar aversion in mind, she offered, "We can make a basic dark chocolate bar with whatever additions you'd like. Fruit, nuts, or something spicy like cayenne, ginger, or turmeric, which also have medicinal properties."

He smiled in appreciation. "That sounds good. What about

dried apricot and anise? Maybe with some pistachios thrown in."

"Huh. That might not taste too bad. Are you sure you haven't done this before?"

"Positive."

His grin made her stomach spin, but she did her best to ignore it as she assembled the ingredients. "First, we start with the chocolate. I roast and process my own cacao beans, but for time's sake, we'll use a batch I already made."

"Do you mind giving me a quick peek at the process? I've never seen raw cacao beans before."

Sadie blinked, surprised by his interest. She'd assumed he'd want to rush the evening, not actually learn anything. "Sure." She showed him the pantry where they kept the burlap sacks filled with the dried beans. "We source all of our chocolate from direct-trade and sustainable farms. Right now, we have beans from Peru, Guatemala, and Brazil, but they can change depending on crop supply or if we find a new source with an interesting variety."

He widened his eyes, clearly impressed. "They remind me of coffee beans. A while back, Vick gave me a tour of his roasting facility, and I met the legendary roaster, Frank Barrie, who is quite the character."

Sadie smiled. Frank used to be the town recluse, and she'd been afraid of him as a child. But when Cassie arrived a few years ago, she managed to break through his crusty exterior, and now he was a beloved member of the community, though he still had his rough edges. Last fall, he'd taken Vick under his wing, training him to handle the bulk of the roasting that supplied The Calendar Café and a homeless shelter in San Francisco that Frank supported. Sadie had visited their operation several times with Lucy, even picking up a few tips for her own process.

"There are a remarkable number of similarities between coffee and chocolate, from how it's farmed to how it's roasted. You know how most dark chocolate is considered bitter?"

"Yeah."

"That's because it's been over roasted. Burned, essentially. But if you roast the beans lighter, you can maintain their natural sweetness and don't need to add as much sugar. Same thing with coffee. If it's over roasted, it will taste bitter, which is why a lot of people compensate with cream and sugar. But with coffee like Frank's, it's so smooth, you can drink it black."

"That's fascinating. I never realized they had so much in common, when on the surface, they're so different." He seemed pleased by the discovery, and Sadie's mind involuntarily drew a parallel between herself and Landon. A parallel she quickly dismissed.

"Of course, don't ask me to explain how it all works," she said with a nervous laugh. "All I know is, I roast the beans in the oven, and they magically release all the delicious flavors and aromas."

"It's called the Maillard reaction," he explained, his dark eyes sparkling with the same passion she'd seen in the restaurant. The mesmerizing sheen reminded her of her favorite Belgian chocolate—deep, rich, and velvety. Her lungs momentarily forgot how to do their job, and she struggled to regain a steady flow of oxygen as he continued. "It's a chemical reaction between the amino acids and reducing sugars as they interact in the heat. At too high or prolonged temperatures, carcinogens called acrylamide can form, which not only affects the taste, but can be dangerous as well."

As she listened to his scientific explanation, a strange

sensation stirred in her stomach. Their two worlds collided, igniting an unexpected connection—and undeniable attraction—as they learned something new from each other. But as tempting as it seemed, what possible future could they have?

She let the sobering thought drag her back to reality. "Wow. I had no idea. I should use that information in my marketing material."

"Feel free. Just don't quote me," he said with a playful chuckle. "So, what happens next?"

She verbally walked him through the rest of the steps, from winnowing to separating the nibs from the shell, to milling, conching, refining, and tempering. As she explained each stage, Landon added a bit of the science behind it, which surprisingly only enhanced the artistic elements.

Art, science, and a little bit of magic came together to produce something she loved. And without Landon's unique perspective, she realized she'd been missing a special piece of her beloved process. Who would've thought Landon Morris would deepen her appreciation and fondness for chocolate?

"I had no idea you used such pure, ethically and sustainably sourced ingredients," he commented as he watched her melt a bar crafted from the finest Peruvian beans.

"That's one thing I've been adamant about since the beginning," she admitted, gratitude swelling in her chest whenever she thought about the many hardworking people involved in the industry. "It all starts with the farmers. What they do is incredibly difficult and labor-intensive, and without them, I wouldn't be able to do what I love. It's important that their work is valued. As the last link in the supply chain, I'm rewarded by the look on customers' faces when they taste a piece of handcrafted chocolate, but honestly, the farmers are the unsung heroes of the trade."

As she spoke, a tender look of admiration and respect crossed Landon's features that made her skin warm and tingly, sparking yet another unexpected realization. They had something else in common—a driving principle to care for people and the planet, an ethos that radiated from every aspect of Landon's business ventures, beginning with the very first product he ever invented.

Faced with the reality of their shared values, and the erratic beating of her heart whenever their gazes met, Sadie needed answers.

Well, one in particular.

And she wouldn't let the evening end without an honest attempt to surmount the wall between them.

Sucking in a deep breath, she blurted out her question before she lost her nerve. "Landon, what's the *real* story behind why you hate sugar?"

His jaw tense, Landon gazed into the melting pot of satiny chocolate, letting her question hang in the sweet-smelling air between them.

Ever since his crusade against sugar began, he'd made a point not to divulge the personal reason behind his vendetta. It wasn't fair to drag his mother into the limelight and expose the raw wounds of her life to the harsh public eye.

Not after all she'd been through already.

But with Sadie, everything felt different. She genuinely cared about his mother, and he'd witnessed her kindness and compassion countless times. He could trust her. And more than that, he actually *wanted* to confide in her—a desire he'd never experienced with anyone before.

He continued to watch the syrupy chocolate swirl as he confessed, "My mom has type 1 diabetes."

"I'm so sorry." Her soft voice exuded empathy, enveloping him in a welcomed warmth like a verbal embrace.

He swallowed against the uncomfortable tightness in his throat threatening to trap his words. "It can be a manageable disease, but my mom always had trouble following the doctor's recommendations. Particularly around her diet and regulating her insulin levels. But it's not entirely her fault," he added as a familiar defensiveness reared its head. "Sugar is in everything. Including supposed health foods. It's exhausting to be cognizant of everything you eat 24-7."

"I can imagine it would be."

Landon appreciated her sincerity, and it gave him the courage to forge ahead. "She was in and out of the hospital a lot, which took a toll on her mental health, which in turn, affected her eating habits since she used sweets as a coping mechanism. When things got really bad, it was like she suddenly stopped caring about her health altogether. To the point where she ignored a minor cut on her leg that led to a serious infection. By the time she sought help, the doctors had no choice but to amputate."

"Oh, how awful," Sadie gasped. She'd taken the chocolate off the burner and let it settle in the pot, their candy-making class completely forgotten.

For a moment, Landon closed his eyes, not wanting to relive the worst time of his life. "I didn't even find out about it until after the surgery. The hospital called because she needed a ride after they discharged her."

"What about your dad?"

Her curiosity was innocent enough, but he couldn't fight

the involuntary wince. "They couldn't reach him, so I was next on her list of emergency contacts."

All the emotions of that afternoon came flooding back—the shock, fear, and confusion. Followed by anger, pain, and intense betrayal when his father's text pinged his phone like a piercing bullet wound. "It turns out they couldn't reach him because he was ignoring their calls."

"Why would he do that?" The question escaped her lips in a wary whisper, as though she was afraid of the answer.

Landon's chest constricted, strangling his response. As he swallowed, his saliva burned his throat. "Because he's a coward." The word, though accurate, tasted acrid on his tongue. "He didn't even have the nerve to tell me, man-to-man. I got a text. *I'm sorry. I can't do this anymore* was all it said. I can't do *this*, as if being a loving and supportive husband was some optional activity you could abandon as soon as it was no longer convenient."

"He left her in the hospital after a major surgery?" Horror and disbelief flickered across her features in equal measure. "How could anyone be so cruel?"

Landon didn't answer. He couldn't. He'd grappled with the same question since the nightmare began and could come up with only one possible conclusion.

Most people—even the ones you thought you could count on—cared more about their own needs and feelings than those of others. Even their supposed loved ones. Deep down, even the most devoted of souls was capable of desertion if pushed too far.

He thought of the letters he'd translated the other day on the way to his meeting in the city. Abélard's agony oozed off the page as he beseeched Lise to come back to him, to not abandon their love. And yet, every single one of his heartfelt messages seemed to disappear into the void, never receiving a response.

Ultimately, they wound up buried beneath layers of plaster and paint, for reasons he couldn't fathom. In light of the tragic outcome, Landon couldn't bring himself to give the letters back to Sadie yet. He'd hoped for a happy ending but had discovered more tragedy. Pain soaked through the aged paper, deeper than the ink itself, reinforcing what he already knew: most love stories didn't last.

He'd need to return the letters eventually, but doing so felt like sealing their own fate, as if they were an omen or warning. And however true that may be, he wasn't ready to face the end of whatever was happening between them.

Sadie waited patiently as he struggled to escape his thoughts. Finally, he gave the only answer that came to mind. "I don't know. I've asked myself the same question ever since. But who can know the mind of someone else? I just focus on the things I can control."

"Like the world's sugar consumption?" she asked softly.

Although he could tell from her tone that she wasn't mocking him, something about the way she phrased the question made something click inside his head, in a way it never had before.

He'd experienced a lot of success in his life, amassing the kind of wealth that made anything seem possible, for the right price. And with the various nonprofits he'd either founded or funded, he'd witnessed tremendous improvements in areas he cared deeply about. But was this one undertaking he never should have attempted?

As if sensing she'd given him a lot to think about, she said, "I'm truly sorry, Landon. I can't even imagine what you've been through. Or what your mom's been through. But I can appreciate, and even admire, the lengths you've gone to try to protect her and others with a similar struggle. And I'm really glad you shared all of this with me." She placed a hand on his forearm, just beneath the rolled cuff of his sweater, and the warmth of her touch at once soothed him and sent his heart racing.

Almost as soon as her fingertips grazed his skin, she retracted her hand, and he immediately missed the feel of her.

She offered a sympathetic smile. "In any other circumstance, I'd offer to make a comforting cup of hot chocolate. But in this case, I think it might have the opposite effect."

"You know what," he said slowly. "Let's give it a try."

Her brows furrowed, revealing her hesitation. "Are you sure?"

"I'm not sure about anything these days. But I'm open to new possibilities," he admitted, silently adding, *In more areas than one.*

CHAPTER 18

As she gathered the ingredients for the hot chocolate, Sadie focused on taking slow, steady breaths, hoping to calm the nervous quiver in her stomach.

She'd never shared her secret recipe with anyone before, apart from Gigi, who'd created the first version of the recipe almost two decades ago. But after Landon poured out his heart, revealing such a private, personal part of himself, she felt compelled to reciprocate somehow.

She set the copper pot on the stove while Landon peered over her shoulder. He stood so close, his spicy cologne mingled with the rich scent of roasted cacao beans, tempting her to distraction.

What was the milk-to-cream ratio again? Her gaze flitted toward the ceiling as she racked her brain for the right measurements.

Come on, Sadie, she mentally scolded herself. *Get it together. You can make hot chocolate in your sleep.*

"I have to admit"—Landon's deep voice hummed in her ear, making her shiver—"during my first visit to Poppy Creek,

I heard about your famous hot cocoa. And even though I avoid sugar, I was curious to know what set it apart from the rest and why everyone raved about it."

She slowly whisked the milk and heavy cream, concentrating on the simmering bubbles dancing across the surface. "First of all, it's hot *chocolate*, not hot cocoa."

"There's a difference?"

She smiled, accustomed to the common misconception. "A big difference. Hot cocoa is made with a powdered mix while hot chocolate requires real melted chocolate, which makes it thick and creamy."

"Huh. I had no idea. I always thought the terms were interchangeable." A teasing quality crept into his voice as he added, "Look at me, learning all sorts of new things tonight."

She didn't dare glance over her shoulder, knowing the sight of his grin would only further muddle her mixed feelings. Her defenses had slipped far enough already, leaving her vulnerable and emotionally unsettled.

"Correct me if I'm wrong," he said thoughtfully, "but don't you sell a powdered version of your hot chocolate? I saw some for sale in The Calendar Café. When I asked Cassie about it, she said it flies off the shelf."

Her hand stilled, and the bubbles coalesced, creating a thick layer of froth. Was it her imagination or had he taken more than a casual interest in her business lately? Was it merely the curiosity of a rival? Or something more personal?

She ignored her quickening pulse. "You're right. I do. I got so many requests from customers who wanted to make the hot chocolate at home, I created a special mix that gives them a close approximation without revealing my secret recipe."

"I see." His dark eyes twinkled. "It's a secret? So, once you show me, you'll have to keep me quiet by any means necessary?"

She laughed despite her fluttering nerves. "Don't worry, I won't hire a hitman. But you will be sworn to secrecy."

He mimed zipping his lips and locking them with an invisible key he then tossed over his shoulder. Normally, she would have found the playful gesture humorous, but she was too fixated on his lips to be amused. Lips that had been so close to meeting her own a few nights ago. She couldn't help but wonder what they tasted like, though she had a feeling they'd be intoxicatingly rich with a satisfying sweetness akin to her exclusive gold-dusted truffle with the triple chocolate ganache center.

Worried he could read her thoughts, she jerked her attention back to the task at hand. "To answer your question, this is what sets my hot chocolate apart from the rest." She reached for a small jar of freshly ground espresso. When she unscrewed the lid, a heady aroma sprang from inside, swirling around them.

"Coffee?" He sounded surprised.

"I only add a pinch to the entire pot, but the espresso intensifies the chocolate flavor."

"What made you think to try the combination?"

"Trial and error. I spent months playing with the recipe. And that was after Gigi spent several weeks perfecting the original version, which tasted heavenly in its own right. But I wanted to add my own spin on it. Sort of as a rite of passage when she handed over the reins of the sweet shop."

"Your grandmother must be really proud of you."

At his words, her breath stalled, slowing her heartbeat. Her entire life, the motivation behind every decision she made, was to make her grandmother proud, to atone for all the sacrifices she'd made in order to raise her. And somehow, this man—who admittedly loathed her livelihood—had spoken the very words that encapsulated her deepest desire.

She turned to look at him, and the soft, simmering heat in his gaze sent a pleasant prickle skittering across her skin.

Against all reason—and quite frankly, her sanity—he had a strange influence over her, a powerful pull that defied her self-control and better judgment. While her mind told her to step back and create distance, her heart was desperate to draw closer, to bridge the gap between them by sharing something intimate.

Before she could change her mind, she blurted, "Gigi isn't technically my grandmother. Not by blood."

"Really? You two seem so alike."

Her heart warmed at his simple comment, as though he'd paid her the highest compliment. "She's raised me since I was nine. When my parents passed away."

His expression immediately sobered; empathy reflected in his eyes. "Sadie, I'm so sorry. That's unbearable to experience at any age, let alone as a child. I'll never forget how I felt the day I got the call from the hospital about my mom. The fear and panic, wondering what they'd say, if I was finally getting *the call* informing me they'd done all they could for her. But I can't even imagine losing both of my parents. And so young. How does a kid cope with the knowledge that their parents are never coming home?"

Tears stung her eyes as he spoke. His words held the familiar pain of someone who understood loss and the weight of her ever-present fear. Although their situations were different, they carried a similar burden. And she found that fact oddly comforting, as though maybe they could carry it—and eventually overcome it—together.

"For a long time, I didn't think I could cope," she confessed, her voice hoarse from the painful memory. "I didn't come out of my room for weeks. I didn't eat or sleep. I felt so alone, even though Gigi had given up her glamorous, globe-trotting life the second she found out about the car accident. At the time, I didn't know her that well. She'd been my maternal grandmother's best friend, but she lived abroad and traveled constantly. When my grandmother died, Gigi stepped in and became a sort of surrogate mother to my mom, who made her my guardian should anything ever happen to them. But I didn't see her all that often. Just received the occasional postcard and souvenir."

"It must have been difficult to lose your parents and then be raised by someone you barely knew."

"It was at first," she admitted, a smile breaking through her tears. "But if you've met Gigi, you know she has the biggest heart. For weeks after the accident, she spent every evening in the kitchen working on a hot chocolate recipe, trying to replicate one she'd tasted at a small café in Paris. She said in France, chocolate is for lovers, but *hot* chocolate is for love that is lost. Liquid comfort, if you will."

"I take it she eventually perfected the recipe?"

"She did. The secret was using both dark and white chocolate, which enhanced the creaminess." Sadie broke two bars of chocolate into small chunks and slowly sprinkled them into the dense milky concoction, watching the contrasting ribbons of color swirl together as she stirred. "When she was finally satisfied with the result, she brought a mug to my room."

Once the chocolate melted, Sadie added a pinch of espresso, then stirred a few more minutes before she poured the satiny mixture into two mugs, savoring the aromatic steam that curled from the rim. She handed one to Landon.

"Something happened when I took my first sip." Tears sprang to her eyes again as visions of that night rose to the surface, overwhelming her with their intensity.

"What happened?" he prompted gently.

She wrapped both hands around the smooth porcelain, as though cradling a priceless antique. "When I tasted the hot chocolate, for the first time since my parents passed away, I had hope. Hope that things would be okay. That *I'd* be okay."

A tear slid down her cheek and she brushed it aside. "Which sounds ridiculous, I know. Who finds hope in something silly like hot chocolate? At the time, I didn't fully understand it. But as I got older, it finally made sense. Gigi had poured her heart and soul into that recipe. She'd gone above and beyond, working tirelessly for nights on end to find a means to comfort me the best way she knew how. And on a deep level, even as a child, I knew with an extraordinary, selfless love like Gigi's, I'd be okay."

When Sadie finished sharing, an acute awareness stole over her, as though she'd just bared her soul and now stood before him naked and exposed. What would he think? What would he say?

For a long moment, neither of them spoke. Raindrops pinged against the window and the world beyond was inky black. In the stillness, everything around them seemed to disappear, leaving them isolated and alone with her confession.

She fought the urge to run and forced herself to meet his gaze.

Her breath caught when he lifted the mug to his lips and took a languid sip.

Time slowed down, nearly stopping altogether as he swallowed.

Landon Morris, the antisugar king, was drinking her hot chocolate.

He lowered the mug, his eyes never leaving her face. "I may disagree with your grandmother on this one," he said, his voice husky.

"What do you mean?" Her heartbeat stammered. Didn't he like it?

"I don't think this hot chocolate is just for lost love. To me, it tastes like a whole lot more than that."

Landon's heart hammered inside his chest, matching the rhythm of the raindrops against the window.

Had he really just said that?

It sounded like a confession. A confession he wasn't ready to make. At least, not out loud.

Before tonight, he'd known he was falling for Sadie. His feelings for her had increased steadily, like liquid heating on a slow simmer. But now, he felt as if someone had turned up the Bunsen burner all the way, and if he wasn't careful, his emotions would boil over.

He needed to regroup. "I guess what I mean is, hot chocolate can represent all forms of love. Like your grandmother's love for you. Although, I can see why it's considered comforting, too."

In fact, he was pretty sure he'd heard her grandmother's expression about hot chocolate being for lost love somewhere else before. He just couldn't remember where....

Normally, he'd revolt at the idea of something sugary and sweet being a comfort food, a way to ease emotional pain. After all, that's partly what contributed to his mother's problems. But something about Sadie's story felt different and his heart softened. Maybe the issue wasn't as black-and-white as he'd initially thought.

In response to his remark, Sadie flashed the kind of smile that made the rest of the world fade away. "For once, I agree with you."

As they stood smiling at each other, something between them shifted, like a barrier had been torn down.

He stepped closer, his gaze fixed on her striking features, captivated by every infinitesimal flicker of emotion—the faint flutter of her eyelashes, the slight parting of her lips, the way her eyes widened when she drew in a breath.

Once again, silky caramel-colored strands had slipped from her ponytail, framing her face. This time, instead of sweeping them aside, he reached for the elastic band confining the rest. Without thinking, he tucked his fingers around it and tugged gently. It slid down the length of her ponytail, and her hair spilled around her shoulders, shimmering in the soft glow of the kitchen.

She inhaled sharply, but didn't look away, arching her neck so her chin tipped toward him.

Emboldened by the gesture, he threaded his fingers through her hair, cupping the back of her head. His pulse raced and heat surged through every fiber in his body, overwhelming his senses with desire and adrenaline.

He lowered his lips toward hers, driven by impulse and need more than logic.

All the scientific formulas and theorems in the world couldn't explain their connection. But he didn't need them to —they simply worked. Somehow, someway, they made each other better. Like espresso and chocolate, together they became something more extraordinary than when they were apart.

A breath away from their first kiss, his heart stopped beating.

The world around them disappeared, completely inconsequential.

But before their lips met, his phone rang, slicing through the moment like a blinding beam of light.

Startled, she stepped back, slipping away from him as sensibility took over.

For several seconds, he couldn't move as he struggled to process the sudden shift.

"You should answer that." She gathered her hair in her hand, ensnaring it with the elastic band.

The resounding snap wrenched all hope from his grasp. Regretfully, he pressed the phone to his ear. "Hello?"

"Are you still with Sadie?" His mother's excited voice buzzed on the other end.

"Yes." He tried to keep his annoyance from creeping into his tone.

"Put me on speaker."

He did as she asked, mouthing *It's my mom* to Sadie, who immediately straightened, collecting herself.

"Guess what?" Irene said by way of greeting, her smile audible.

Before either of them could answer, she announced, "I have a date to the Valentine's Day Dance."

"You do?" Sadie brightened. "Don't tell me. It's Bill Tucker, isn't it?"

"You are correct." His mother sounded like a giddy teenager before her first prom. "Which means, I need to go dress shopping. And I'd like you to go with me."

"I'd love to."

"Wonderful! Then I need you both to take the day off tomorrow, if possible. I don't think I'll find what I'm looking for in Poppy Creek."

"What'd you have in mind?" Landon asked, though he didn't need convincing to spend the entire day with Sadie.

"My favorite store, of course. That is, if you don't mind. It's a bit out of the way."

"I don't mind at all," Landon assured her, grinning at the thought. "In fact, I think it's perfect."

CHAPTER 19

Even after the long flight in Landon's luxurious private jet, Sadie couldn't believe she was sitting inside a designer boutique on the famed Fifth Avenue in New York City. She had to be dreaming! But the glass of champagne in her hand and tray of extravagant hors d'oeuvres featuring exclusive offerings like beluga caviar, Somerset cheddar, and French truffles—not to mention the array of thousand-dollar dresses hand-selected by a team of personal shoppers—said otherwise.

"What do you think?" Irene breezed out of the dressing room wearing a silvery chiffon evening gown with sheer sleeves and delicate beadwork decorating the snug bodice. The light, ethereal color contrasted beautifully with her dark hair and eyes and highlighted the pink tinge of her cheeks.

She'd always been an attractive woman, but there had been something haunting about her beauty, like an abandoned mansion, once stunning and full of life left to slowly crumble from neglect.

"You look breathtaking," Sadie told her sincerely, her throat tightening at the sight.

Irene's metamorphosis, which began on the inside and radiated outward, touched a hidden place in Sadie's heart. If she were honest, she longed for a similar transformation, if only to feel truly at peace with herself.

At her compliment, Irene's blush deepened. The woman had never looked happier. In a relatively short time, she'd found a long-forgotten confidence and returned to a boutique she'd frequented before her surgery. And even though her experience had changed, and she now needed help to try on the glamorous gowns, it hadn't dampened her spirits.

Not for the first time, Sadie marveled at the impact one person could have on another. A kind word, an offer of friendship, an extension of trust. A small act could have a tremendous outcome, one that inevitably had a ripple effect.

Sadie stole a glance at Landon, who sat beside her on the ridiculously plush settee that could've been plucked from Buckingham Palace.

Something in his expression—a tender blend of astonishment and affection—roused tears she'd held at bay. Blinking rapidly, she looked away.

While he'd never verbalized the desire in so many words, she'd sensed how desperately he longed to see his mother happy and whole. The watery glint in his eyes revealed the magnitude of the moment.

"Sadie's right, Mom," he murmured, his voice rough with emotion. "You look beautiful."

"Thank you, sweetheart." Irene gazed at her reflection in the trifold mirror, her own countenance a mixture of pleasure and disbelief. "You don't think it's too much?"

"Not at all," Sadie assured her, though her own attire for

the dance paled in comparison. She'd worn the same black cocktail dress to nearly every formal event in the past three years. It wasn't fancy, but at least it was flattering. Plus, it wasn't like she had the time—or the financial means—to shop for anything new. And certainly not anything she'd find hanging in a shop like this one. "Honestly, Irene, it's perfect. Bill is going to be speechless when he sees you in it."

"I do like to leave a man tongue-tied." Irene flashed a girlish grin, then turned to the tall, stately attendant standing off to the side. "I'll take it."

The woman—a picture of professionalism in her crisp yet stylish pantsuit—paired her nod with an approving smile. "Excellent choice. I'll have the hem altered while you try on some matching heels."

Sadie waited for Irene's reaction, wondering if she'd insist on keeping the length and decline the fancy footwear, revisiting her former insecurities.

Instead, Irene asked, "You don't happen to offer half off if I only need one shoe, do you?" Her laugh was rich and throaty, filled with good-natured humor without the dark cloud of self-deprecation. Such a stark contrast to her previous inhibitions, further highlighting the positive effect of her newfound friendships. Not to mention her budding romance with Bill.

"I'll see what I can do." The attendant responded with jovial warmth before summoning her assistant with a flourish of her long, expertly manicured fingers. She rattled off a few designer names Sadie didn't recognize, along with Irene's shoe size and preferred styles.

The younger woman—who could easily be a runway model for a couture fashion line—scuttled off with all the enthusiasm of a little girl accessorizing her Barbie doll.

Sadie settled deeper into the settee and sipped her champagne, blissfully content with the events of the evening thus far. Soon, they'd be exploring the vibrant, boisterous streets, basking in the brilliant glow of the city lights while breathing in the infectious energy that zipped through the air like an electrical current. At the mere thought of finally fulfilling a lifelong dream, anticipation pulsed through her, scattering goose bumps across her skin.

"Sadie," Irene cut in, drawing her back to the present, "it's your turn."

"For what?"

"To try on dresses."

Sadie's mouth fell open, her throat dry. "Oh, no. I'm only here for moral support. I already know what I'm wearing to the dance."

"And I'm sure it's lovely. But won't you indulge me by trying on one or two dresses while we're here?" Irene pursed her lips in a persuasive pout. "Please? It'll be fun."

Fun? Sadie ran a clammy palm down her jean-clad thigh. Modeling gowns she couldn't afford sounded like the opposite of fun. Especially with Landon in the audience. Her limbs turned limp beneath his gaze under normal circumstances. How could she survive purposefully placing herself under his appraising eyes?

As if on cue, the older attendant produced a rolling rack bursting with Oscar-worthy gowns that just so happened to be in Sadie's size.

Clearly, Irene had planned ahead.

Sadie swallowed a gulp of champagne, hoping to dislodge the lump of apprehension stuck in her throat.

No such luck.

She slowly set down the glass, her heart racing.

Irene looked so hopeful, so happy. How could she say no?

She managed a slight smile. "Okay. I suppose one or two wouldn't hurt."

On wobbly legs, she accompanied the attendant to the dressing room, mindful of Landon watching every step she took.

Why did his attentive gaze both thrill and intimidate her?

The second Sadie emerged from the dressing room Landon experienced a scientific anomaly. Time stood motionless, preserving the moment, as if knowing he needed a few extra minutes to savor the sight of her.

Barefoot and timid, she tiptoed forward, holding the hem of the dress in both hands. The silky red fabric cascaded over every curve as though she'd been dipped in a candy apple coating.

He resisted the urge to shrug out of his coat and strip down to his undershirt thanks to the sudden spike in his body temperature.

Get it together, man. Breathe. Blink. And whatever you do, don't gawk.

Avoiding his gaze, she stepped in front of the full-length mirror and studied her reflection as though observing a stranger. "It's not really my style."

"I don't know what you're talking about. You took phenomenal," Irene gushed. "That dress was made for you." Her mouth twisted into an impish smile as she turned to him and asked, "Don't you agree?"

Was it his imagination or did Sadie's complexion suddenly turn several shades rosier?

He cleared his throat, attempting to project a casual

demeanor as he took in her appearance, despite the erratic cadence of his heartbeat. "It looks great."

Great? Great? His own words echoed in his ear, undoubtedly the understatement of the millennium.

"It's a beautiful dress." Sadie smoothed invisible wrinkles in the skirt, drawing attention to the way it hugged her hips.

He cringed when his mother caught him staring.

She flashed him a knowing grin before turning to Sadie. "I'd like to buy it for you, if I may. As a thank-you for everything you've done for me."

"Oh, no. I couldn't let you do that," Sadie said hastily. "Besides, you don't owe me a thank-you."

Irene readied for a rebuttal, but before she could press further, Sadie hopped off the pedestal. "Is anyone else starving? Can we get something quick to eat before we head back? I think we passed a falafel cart on the way here."

"Actually," Irene began with a mischievous lilt, "there's something I've been meaning to ask you both." She glanced in his direction, her dark eyes twinkling. "An old friend invited me to dinner, but I realize that would mean we won't get home until late. Is that all right with you two?"

"I don't mind. We can always sleep on the plane," Sadie said with an understanding smile.

Landon shot his matchmaking mother a look, but she ignored him. "Thank you, dear. I shouldn't be too long, and Landon can give you a mini tour of the city before we leave."

"I'd like that." For the first time since she exited the dressing room, Sadie met his eye. Her sweet, unassuming smile left him winded. Good thing he was already sitting down. "If it's not too much trouble," she added.

"Not at all," he assured her, somehow finding his voice. "There is one place in particular I'd like to take you."

He already had it all planned out. And it was the perfect spot to finally tell her how he felt.

That is, if he could muster the courage.

CHAPTER 20

Landon watched Sadie closely, holding his breath as he waited for her reaction.

"The Empire State Building?" Her eyes wide and glittering, she gazed up at the towering behemoth. An enormous red heart shone on the side like a brilliant beacon in celebration of Valentine's Day later that week.

"I know it's touristy, but you can't visit New York without seeing the view from the top."

"We're going to the top?" Her entire countenance gleamed brighter than Times Square.

"Yep." He grinned, barely able to contain his own excitement as she snapped a few photos with her phone.

Not that he'd admit it, but after their movie night, he'd devoured every film starring Tom Hanks and Meg Ryan, including *Sleepless in Seattle,* which concluded with an iconic scene at the top of the Empire State Building. On Valentine's Day, no less. While he'd never considered himself to be much of a romantic, particularly not in the past few years, since meeting Sadie, he wanted to believe in happily ever afters.

He thought about Abélard. The poor man had fought hard for his happy ending. Too bad it hadn't worked out. Although, perhaps there was more to the story than the letters revealed.

With any luck, they would find out soon.

After Sadie mentioned her desire to learn more about the man behind the letters, Landon enlisted the help of a friend who was developing special software for the government. In theory, it could locate just about anyone. While it wasn't meant for the general public, Landon made him an offer he couldn't refuse. If all went well, he'd be able to give Sadie the letters *and* info on Abélard.

The prospect of surprising her with the extra information made his heart swell. He considered himself a generous person who enjoyed doing things for others, but nothing brought him more joy than making Sadie smile. Most women he'd dated expected lavish gifts and extravagant outings. They'd coveted the perks of being with a billionaire more than they'd cared about him as a person.

Then he'd met Sadie. Unpretentious and unassuming, she worked hard and didn't take anything for granted. And she certainly hadn't gone out of her way to ingratiate herself or ply him for favors. In fact, she'd done the opposite, butting heads with him on too many occasions to count.

He chuckled inwardly, recalling some of their feisty exchanges. She held her own and stood by her principles, even when they opposed his own, and he admired her strength of character.

He watched her angle her phone, capturing the full scope of the steel-framed skyscraper. Her eyes held all the awe and amazement of someone glimpsing an indescribable wonder for the first time. He could get used to seeing the world through her eyes.

Once she'd collected several shots of the building and surrounding streets, she moved to join the mob of tourists in line for the observation deck.

"This way." He placed a hand on her lower back, directing her around the crowd. Even with the barrier of his gloves and her thick jacket, the brief contact made his pulse race.

"Don't we have to wait in line?"

"Nope."

"Let me guess. You know a guy?" she teased.

"Something like that." With a playful grin, he pushed through the revolving door.

He led her to the first elevator. Inside the cocooned space, heat radiated between them. The sweet, ambrosial scent of her perfume settled around him, kicking his pulse up another notch.

Get it together, man.

Her presence had a way of sending him off-kilter, muddling his emotions until he could hardly think straight.

But tonight, he wanted to remain fully cognizant, cementing every detail in his mind.

After a series of elevators, they navigated a cramped passageway.

"Where exactly are we going?" Sadie scanned their unusual surroundings, taking in the dusty electrical boxes and copper piping with a confused frown. The crease in her brow deepened as they approached a steep, narrow stairwell.

"You'll see. We're almost there." He maintained an air of mystery, eagerly anticipating her reaction when they reached the final summit.

Not many people knew about the exclusive 103rd floor located in the metal mast at the top of the tower. And when they emerged onto the tiny balcony with no more than a knee-high ledge separating them from the dizzying heights, the breathtaking view drew an audible gasp from her lips.

Below them, the city shimmered against an obsidian backdrop like the night sky turned upside down. Major motorways crisscrossed like gilded streams and star-studded skyscrapers converged to create a picture-perfect panorama, rendered even more beautiful thanks to the company beside him.

"What do you think?" Despite the enthralling cityscape, he couldn't take his eyes off Sadie's face. Her cheeks glowed from the cold, caressed by soft wisps of hair tossed about by the wind.

"It's the most stunning sight I've ever seen." She moved closer to the edge, undeterred by the precarious platform. "Where are we?"

"The 103rd floor, just below the antenna."

"I never even knew this place existed."

"That's because it's not open to the public."

She turned to look at him, both amazed and amused. "You live in a completely different world from the rest of us, don't you?"

What could he say? That he didn't want to live in any world that didn't include her? Instead, he merely shrugged.

She turned back to admire the view, and for a long moment, they stood side by side, not saying a word, merely taking in the striking tableau.

A biting gust of wind whipped past them, and Sadie shivered.

"Cold?" he asked.

"A little. But I'm not ready to leave yet. I don't think I'll ever be ready to leave."

He strode toward a small rolling cart situated off to the

side, eager for phase two of the evening. "I have something that should warm you up." His heart thrummed inside his chest as he pulled the lever on the silver urn and thick, creamy liquid poured into the paper cup. Steam rose from the rim, tickling his senses with its rich scent.

Her eyes widened as he handed her the cup. "Hot chocolate?" Her voice carried a mixture of delight and disbelief.

"From a small café that originated in Paris. It became so popular, they expanded to New York." He didn't want to admit how much research he'd put into finding it, but after what she'd shared about her grandmother, he wanted her to experience authentic French hot chocolate. "It's named after a woman, but it's slipping my mind at the moment. Andrea's... Angelica's..."

"Angelina's?"

"That's the name! You've heard of it?"

Her features softened, taking on a faraway, wistful expression. She took a sip, savoring it for several seconds before whispering, "This is it."

"What?"

"The hot chocolate that inspired Gigi's recipe. It has to be." Tears glistened in her eyes. "I can't believe it."

Landon stared, too stunned to speak. He'd wanted to surprise her with genuine Parisian hot chocolate, but he had no clue it would be *the* hot chocolate.

What could be more serendipitous?

He regarded the array of emotions flickering across her features, captivated by the depth of feeling conveyed in each subtle movement. With every sip she swallowed, an idea became even more ingrained in his mind.

Impulsively, he blurted, "That's what you should enter in the Tastiest Treat competition."

"What?" she asked, slowly coming out of her reverie.

"Your hot chocolate."

She smiled. "That's a sweet thought, but it's far too simple. As good as it is, it won't impress the judges."

"What if you jazzed it up? You could combine your recipe with some molecular gastronomy techniques."

"Maybe. But I don't know anything about molecular gastronomy."

"I do."

She met his gaze, her eyes questioning. "What exactly are you saying?"

He gathered a breath. "What if I help you?"

"You would do that?"

"I don't know if you've noticed, but I would do just about anything for you, Sadie Hamilton."

His words hung in the air between them, leaving him painfully exposed. He didn't like being vulnerable, preferring to be in charge and in control. But a chance at winning Sadie's heart was worth risking his own.

She didn't respond, and his erratic heartbeat echoed in the excruciating silence.

But he'd come too far to give up now. And he wanted her too badly. "I know it doesn't make sense. We're the least-obvious couple in the world. And we'd probably drive each other crazy. But I can't help thinking we'd also be perfect together. And if you'd give me a chance, I—"

Before he could say another word, she stepped toward him.

Her arms encircled his neck as her lips met his, drawing him into a kiss unlike anything he'd ever experienced before.

As he pulled her against him, something deep within ignited like a spark, and each soft moan and caress of her fingertips acted like an accelerant, setting his entire body ablaze. Not even the biting wind penetrating his coat could squelch the intense heat between them, and he'd stand on that ledge forever if it meant never letting her go.

Hot chocolate may have given Sadie hope, but for him, he'd found it in her kiss.

~

Moved by Landon's gesture, Sadie gave herself over to the moment, to every impulse she'd fought for the last several days.

She didn't want to think or even feel anything beyond the sensation of his strong body firmly melded against hers, the warmth of his skin beneath her fingertips, the taste of his lips.

For the time being, they weren't Sadie and Landon, polar opposites who owned competing businesses. They lived in another world, one where nothing mattered except for here and now. Desire and immediacy triumphed over reason.

But her delicious delusions couldn't last forever, and the not-so-subtle whispers of her fears and insecurities wormed their way into her thoughts.

You may think this is what you want, but deep down, you know it will only end in heartache. Be strong. The risk isn't worth the regret.

With one hand on his chest, she broke away, breathing heavily. "I'm sorry. I can't."

"What's wrong?" His gaze bored into hers, the glint of longing dampened by uncertainty.

Pained, she looked away. "It's not you, it's—" She winced, despising the hollow cliché. How had she let this happen?

This was her fault. She'd made the first move, and now she'd made a mess of everything.

Her head throbbed as panic and confusion surged through her, and for the first time that night, she found the height dizzying.

What she wouldn't give to rewind and undo her mistake.

"Can—can we pretend this never happened?" she whispered, too ashamed to meet his gaze.

"No, we can't." He reached for her hand, his expression earnest, hopeful. "Sadie, I—"

"Please, Landon." She took a step back, creating a chasm that spanned more than the physical.

An unbearable silence followed, and when he finally spoke, the hurt in his voice cut through her. "If that's what you want."

Even as she nodded, she couldn't help wondering...

Was this what she wanted?

CHAPTER 21

The next few days plodded by in a procession of slow, painful seconds. Nothing could lift Sadie's spirits, not even the uptick in sales thanks to last-minute Valentine's Day shoppers. During a time when her sole focus should be saving the shop and rejoicing with each *ding* of the cash register, her thoughts lingered on Landon. And their kiss.

No matter how desperately she tried, she couldn't deny their connection. And despite herself, she even understood his hatred of sugar, however misguided.

But could she ignore reality? They were on opposite sides, too rooted in their beliefs to change. Even if she wanted things to work out between them, it simply wasn't possible. Not in the long run.

Confused and conflicted, she stared blankly at the TV screen. Reruns of *Murder, She Wrote* usually provided a pleasant distraction from her troubles, but tonight she couldn't concentrate. The *tick, tick, tick* of the grandfather clock served as a constant reminder of the evening she'd gone out of her way to avoid.

If Gigi were home instead of visiting a sick friend in Primrose Valley, she would've cajoled her into attending the Valentine's Day Dance. Sadie could almost hear her adamant voice declaring, *We don't run from difficult situations. Like the time I stared down that bull in Pamplona, we face our challenges head-on.*

Of course, Sadie wasn't convinced Gigi had *actually* stared down an irate bovine. Then again, she wouldn't put it past her grandmother, either. Regardless, Gigi wouldn't stand by while Sadie hid from her problems. Which is why she'd breathed a sigh of relief when Gigi announced she'd be gone for a couple of days.

After her lapse in sanity at the top of the Empire State Building, she couldn't face Landon. Especially not at an event as romantic as the Valentine's Day Dance. Ever since their disconcerting encounter, she'd vacillated between regretting her decision to denounce their kiss and doubling down. If she had to endure the enchantment and charm of the dance, she'd tip dangerously toward the former.

She gathered a deep breath and slowly released it, stealing another glance at the clock. The dance wouldn't officially start for a few more hours.

It was going to be a long night....

After refilling her gigantic bowl of comfort popcorn, she settled in for another episode, but before she'd made it through the opening credits, someone hammered on the front door.

Startled, she launched a handful of popped kernels halfway across the room.

BonBon and Truffle bounded after them, and Sadie rushed to collect the carb-laden snack before the already hefty cats got their paws on them.

She stuffed the kernels in the pocket of her bathrobe as she answered the door.

A bundle of excited energy, Lucy bounced on her toes, brandishing a garment bag and a professional-looking hair and makeup kit.

"What are you doing here?" Sadie asked in surprise.

"We're getting ready for the dance together," Lucy said with the air of someone stating the obvious as she waltzed past her.

"Didn't you get my text?"

"You mean the one where you said you weren't going tonight? That was clearly a joke. And not one of your better ones, I might add."

Sadie suppressed a groan. She should've known she couldn't get out of the dance so easily. Although, a part of her had hoped Lucy would've been too distracted by her first Valentine's Day with Vick.

"Sorry, but it wasn't a joke. I'm not going."

"Why not? Are you sick?" Lucy eyed her frayed bathrobe and haphazard bun held in place by a scrunchie she'd owned since middle school.

"Not exactly."

"Then what?" Lucy unloaded her belongings on the coffee table and flounced onto the couch, crossing her long legs. "Spill it. Whatever the reason, it can't be bad enough for you to miss the dance."

With a sigh, Sadie flopped onto the cushion beside her. "I'd rather not talk about it."

"And I'd rather not pluck my eyebrows, but the benefits are worth the discomfort. So, spill."

Sadie squirmed, her resolve wavering.

Lucy leaned forward, studying her with a penetrating

squint, as though she could read Sadie's mind if she tried hard enough. "This is about Landon, isn't it?"

"No!" Sadie responded too quickly, a dead giveaway. *Drat.*

"It is! I knew it." Lucy snapped her fingers in triumph. "What happened?"

Reluctantly, Sadie divulged the details, pausing for Lucy's frequent squeals and exclamations.

When she finally reached the end of her story, revealing how she'd asked Landon to pretend like their kiss never happened, Lucy gasped.

"Why on earth did you do that?"

"Because." Knowing her one-word response wouldn't be sufficient, Sadie recited all the reasons she'd been accumulating for days. "For starters, we can hardly be in the same room for two seconds without arguing. We're too different. And before you say anything, I'm not just talking about our rival businesses, although that's a big part of it." She thought about his offer to help her with the Tastiest Treat competition and wondered what life would be like if she agreed. Did he still plan on entering his Strawberry Shortcake Cloud? And what about his shop? Would they still be in direct competition with each other? How exactly did he foresee that playing out? She had too many questions and not enough answers.

"It's our personalities, too," she continued, her heart sinking further and further as she rattled off her list. "And our values. The way we see the world. It's everything. We would never work."

Lucy didn't look convinced. And if she were honest, she wasn't sure she believed her excuses, either. Or more accurately, she didn't *want* to believe them. "Besides," she added for good measure, for her own sake as well as Lucy's. "I don't want to date anyone. I'm perfectly content being on my own. I have more freedom being single."

"To do what?"

"What do you mean?" Sadie frowned, not following.

"This freedom that's so important to you, what do you plan on doing with it?"

"Well... you know..." She waved her hand as if the obscure gesture explained everything.

"No, I don't know. You're going to have to spell it out for me. Because the way I see it, for someone who values freedom, you're the most regimented person I know. You work constantly. You never go on vacation or travel, and your idea of spontaneity is occasionally straying from your standard coffee order. In fact..." Her eyes widened as though she'd just made an important discovery. "Since you've been spending time with Landon, you've come alive. You've traveled and opened yourself up to new and exciting experiences."

Although Sadie was loath to admit it, Lucy had a point. Her life did seem richer over the last several days. More... fulfilling. Had she been too caught up in her roller coaster of emotions to notice?

"You've even let Tracey take on more responsibility at the shop," Lucy continued. "I've never seen you take so much time off. And you went from being obsessed with the Tastiest Treat competition to hardly mentioning it."

Sadie winced. Another valid point. Only this time, it wasn't in her favor.

She'd let her responsibilities slip, and she wasn't proud of it. With so much at stake, she should have buckled down not slacked off. To her chagrin, she'd taken her eyes off of what was really important—saving the shop.

More confused than ever, Sadie rested her head in her

hands, pressure building behind her temples. What should she do?

Another knock at the door interrupted her thoughts.

"Want me to get it?" Lucy offered.

"That's okay." Sadie rose, her muscles stiff with tension.

When she opened the door, she spotted an unfamiliar car disappearing down the driveway.

That's odd....

Even more strange, a plain, rectangular box sat by the welcome mat. Curious, she carried it inside.

"Who was it?" Lucy asked.

"I don't know, but they left this." She rejoined Lucy on the couch, resting the package on her lap. Her heart hummed as she lifted the glossy lid.

Too stunned to speak, she gaped at a silky red dress nestled in crisp white tissue paper.

The same red dress she'd tried on at the boutique in New York.

Her thoughts immediately flew to Landon. Had he purchased it for her? And if so, what did it mean? Her heart beat faster as she flipped open the small note card.

She'd expected to see Landon's neat, even script, but the letters were soft and sloping.

You helped me face my fears and insecurities and take a chance on someone. You helped me take a chance on myself.

Maybe I can do the same for you.

Love,

Irene

. . .

Hot tears hid behind her eyes as she stared at the note, the words blurring into each other. For a brief moment, she wondered if this was what it felt like to have a mother again, someone to gently push her past her comfort zone, to speak tender truths into her life.

Thoughtfully, she caressed the delicate fabric of the gown.

She had a decision to make… between the sensible choice and following her heart.

But which one should she choose?

~

Landon stood in the corner of the room, his melancholy mood clashing with the merriment. All around him, smiling couples danced and mingled, their lighthearted banter and laughter accompanied by lively music.

So far, the band's set list included famous love songs from every decade, but no matter the lyrics, they all seemed to convey the same thing: *You blew it, buddy. You were so close to finding the kind of love musicians write about, but you let it slip through your fingers.*

The lead vocalist belted out the words to "Can't Buy Me Love," and Landon could've sworn the guy looked right at him. And he didn't miss the irony.

He hid a groan behind a gulp of sparkling cider. Why had he let his mother talk him into coming tonight?

Grant sidled up beside him, his face glowing from exertion. He'd spent most of the night whisking Eliza around the dance floor with professional-level skill. "Your mom sure looks happy."

A pang of guilt pierced Landon's chest as he followed Grant's gaze.

Thanks to the best wheelchair money could buy, his mother managed some impressive maneuvers, spinning and swaying, her head thrown back in laughter as Bill busted out his "disco finger," John Travolta–style. Landon had to hand it to the guy; he was surprisingly light on his feet for a man the size of Paul Bunyan.

His mom *did* look happy. Unbelievably so. And the sight should have been more than enough to lift his spirits. After all, this was everything he'd wanted—to see his mother thrive again. Couldn't he put aside his own troubles for a few hours in order to enjoy the evening with her?

"You okay?" Grant asked, rolling up the sleeves of his dress shirt.

"Yeah. I'm fine." Landon straightened and threw his shoulders back, determined to at least pretend he was having a good time.

"Are you sure? You've barely left this corner since you got here. And you keep scanning the room like you're looking for someone."

Landon cringed. Was it that obvious? He hadn't seen Sadie all night and could only assume she was avoiding him, which admittedly stung.

"Relax." Grant slapped a hand against his back. "She'll be here. The night's only just begun."

"Who?" Landon feigned innocence, although he wasn't sure why. Grant had a knack for seeing through his facade.

His friend cracked a grin. "I hate to break it to you, but the whole town knows you're smitten with Sadie."

Rolling his eyes toward the ceiling, Landon groaned. Could things get any worse?

"But don't worry. Only a few of us know the truth."

"What do you mean?"

Grant's features softened. "You should tell her."

"Tell her what?"

Before Grant could respond, the giant barn door swung on its hinges, drawing their attention.

Sadie stood in the doorway, a striking silhouette against the moonlight.

She wore the same red dress she'd tried on in the Fifth Avenue boutique. The one that made his heart race. Only this time, instead of her usual ponytail, her hair fell in shimmering strands around her bare shoulders, brushing her collarbones.

For a moment, Landon couldn't breathe.

Grant nudged him, saying softly, "You should tell her that you love her."

CHAPTER 22

Her heart fluttering wildly, Sadie scanned the room.

The rustic red barn had never looked more beautiful. Strands of soft twinkle lights threaded through the rafters and garlands of fragrant roses and eucalyptus wound around the rough-hewn beams. Olivia had really outdone herself with this event, transforming the simple space into a floral wonderland.

She spotted Lucy and Vick on the dance floor. The love and elation radiating from her friend's face brightened the entire room. At the sight, a knot in Sadie's stomach twisted. She'd resisted love her entire life, convinced she could keep her heart safe, wrapped in a cocoon completely under her control. But something had changed. *She'd* changed. And for the first time, she believed the reward was greater than the risk.

There was just one problem: She might have ruined her only chance.

Her nerves mounted as she searched the crowd for

Landon. When she caught sight of his mother instead, Sadie's heart swelled. Irene looked gorgeous in the silvery gown, her chocolate-brown hair twisted into a simple chignon. Bill handed her a glass of water from the refreshment table, and both of their faces glowed with happiness.

As if sensing her presence, Irene glanced in her direction and smiled. The kind of smile a mother bestowed on a daughter. The kind of smile that said, *I knew you'd come, and I'm so proud of you.*

Sadie swept a hand down the bodice of her dress and mouthed *Thank you*, though the words felt so inadequate. Her gratitude extended far beyond the gown, to depths that couldn't be fully expressed. Yet somehow, she knew Irene understood.

After mouthing *You're welcome* in return, Irene tipped her head toward the far corner of the room.

Sadie followed her gaze, her breath catching at the sight of Landon striding straight for her. His body moved with intent and purpose, the expensive-looking fabric of his graphite-gray suit melded to his strong frame, making her pulse run wild. She'd always considered him to be attractive, albeit begrudgingly at first. But now that she knew him, and had intimate knowledge of his character, she found him downright irresistible.

He stopped a few inches in front of her, so close his spicy cologne spanned the divide, teasing her senses. "You look incredible."

"So do you." She parted her lips to say more, but her thoughts were a jumble, at once coming too fast and not quickly enough. What did she want to say? *I'm sorry? Forgive me, I was wrong? I've missed you?* All of the above?

He smiled as if he could read her mind, and before she could speak another word, he asked, "Would you like to dance?"

The tender timbre of his voice made her limbs tremble slightly. "I'd love to."

She slid her hand in his, relishing the warmth and pressure of his touch as he led her onto the dance floor while the band played "Only Fools Rush In."

Something about the way he drew her into his arms, tucking her against his chest as if he'd never let her go, assured her that her regrettable words atop the Empire State Building had been forgotten.

As the vocalist's mellifluous voice made magic out of the familiar melody, Sadie surrendered to the moment, immersing herself in every single spine-tingling sensation. Each song blurred into the next, and she wasn't sure how much time had passed when a hush fell over the room, followed by collective gasps and murmurings.

She lifted her head, following the enraptured gaze of the crowd toward the center of the dance floor where Reed had dropped to one knee in front of Olivia. Her friend covered her mouth with both hands, her eyes huge and sparkling as Reed removed a small velvet box from his suit jacket.

"Liv," Reed began, transfixed on her face as though they were the only two people in existence. "Ever since we were kids, I knew there was something special about you. You were quiet and shy, yet you had this infectious sweetness about you. I could spend every second of the day with you, even if we were simply lying in the grass gazing up at the clouds, and it still wasn't enough. It didn't take long to realize I wanted to spend the rest of my life by your side." Reed paused, his voice growing husky. "I missed my chance once, and I thought I'd lost you forever. I won't make that mistake again."

He plucked the ring from its resting place, holding it up in the light. From where she stood, Sadie could just make out the lavender hue of the large center stone. "Olivia, you stole my heart a long time ago, and I never want it back. Will you do me the honor of being my wife as well as my best friend?"

Tears welled in Sadie's eyes as her friend nodded, too moved to speak as Reed slid the ring on her finger. On cue, the band began playing "La Vie en Rose" while multicolored rose petals floated down from the ceiling like sweetly perfumed confetti.

Amid cheers and applause, Reed kissed his fiancée then pulled her against him, swaying to the music as other couples joined in.

"I can't believe I almost missed this," Sadie murmured as Landon drew her into his arms again.

"I'm glad you didn't."

Although a simple statement, Sadie knew the subtext ran so much deeper than his words. If she hadn't shown up tonight, she would have missed a whole lot more than her friend's proposal. She nestled her cheek against Landon's shoulder, letting the lyrics wash over her, though she didn't fully understand the French phrases. "I've always loved this song, but I have no idea what it's about."

Landon listened for a moment, then sang softly, "When he holds me in his arms and whispers to me, I see life through rose-colored glasses… the pain and bothers fade away, happy, so happy… it's only him for me and me for him for the rest of our lives…"

Landon's words, though merely quoting a song, spilled into her soul, making her shiver.

Never had lyrics rang truer.

And the realization both thrilled and troubled her.

I *see life through rose-colored glasses....*

A few weeks ago, those lyrics would've been lost on Landon. In fact, he'd viewed life in contrasts of black and white. Mostly black. In his eyes, the world was full of problems to be solved. Nothing was as it should be, and with his wealth and influence, he carried a personal burden to set things right as much as he could.

Now, he saw things differently.

With Sadie, life had a decidedly rosy tinge. Things weren't perfect, and he still felt responsible to make a difference whenever possible, but she'd helped him look at life through a lens of hope. And he'd never seen anything more beautiful.

Lost in the scent of her hair, Landon lightly stroked the soft strands trailing down her back as they slow danced. Though they were once at odds, clashing on a continual basis, holding Sadie in his arms felt like the most natural thing in the world. Despite their differences, he'd been drawn to her from the start, as if his heart had known something his mind had yet to discover.

While to his rational mind, it seemed far too early to consider anything as permanent as marriage, watching Reed propose to Olivia stirred something deep within him—a desire to start a life with Sadie.

He'd never shared so much of himself with anyone before. He'd never told anyone about his mother or what happened with his father. But he knew he could trust her. With his own heart and his mother's. She cared for them both, which meant more to him than he could ever articulate.

In the past, her profession and personal values would've been a deal breaker. But in his heart of hearts, he knew one thing to be true:

Sadie Hamilton was a keeper.

CHAPTER 23

Sadie glanced around the kitchen of the sweet shop, smiling in amusement. Landon's glass beakers and Bunsen burners sat alongside her melangeur and molds, transforming the familiar space into a Willy Wonka–esque laboratory.

Even though they'd been working on her entry for the Tastiest Treat competition all day, she still had to pinch herself. Landon Morris—her unabashed rival—had unexpectedly become her savior. Thanks to his molecular gastronomy techniques, she was confident her hot chocolate would win the contest, giving her the boost she needed to pull herself out of debt and save her shop.

She still couldn't believe it. And yet, here they were.

Landon lifted the steaming beaker carefully, his dark eyes glinting with excitement. "As we pour the cream over the chocolate sphere in the bottom of the glass, the outer shell will melt and release the ingredients inside along with a vapor that tastes like chocolate."

Sadie watched, enthralled as the magic unfolded exactly as

he described. "You forgot to mention the aroma." The intoxicating scent rose from the rim with an intensity so rich, she could already taste it.

He grinned, pleased by her reaction. "Next, we top it with a dollop of marshmallow foam followed by a sprinkle of caramel crystals. And voilà!" He took a step back, beaming proudly.

"I have to admit, it looks incredible." The decadent creation in the tall vintage glass was a piece of art. But would it taste as good as it looked?

"Ready to try it?" He turned the curved handle toward her, giving the glass a nudge.

Suddenly nervous, she slowly lifted it to her lips. What if it tasted terrible? Would she have the heart to tell him?

Ignoring the whispers of doubt, she took a tentative sip. Thick and creamy, the mixture coated her taste buds, bursting with flavor that was at once familiar and delightfully different. How could something taste so rich and dense yet also lighter than air? She couldn't explain it, but the combination was spectacular. Even better than she imagined.

As soon as she swallowed, she brought the glass back to her lips, eager for more. She had a strange, incongruent urge to both gulp down every last drop and slowly savor each sip. She moaned softly.

"That good, huh?"

"I hope you realize you just guaranteed yourself a loss at the Sips & Sweets Festival tomorrow."

"Well, if I had to lose to someone, I'm glad it's you." He leaned in for a kiss, taking his time. When he pulled back—leaving her weak-kneed and breathless—he smacked his lips. "Hey, it does taste pretty good."

She swatted his arm, and the sound of his laugh made her

chest ache in the best possible way. He captured her mouth again, his fingertips caressing the sensitive contour of her cheekbone, trailing down her neck until they threaded through her hair. At every delicate touch, her skin tingled, craving more. Could this really be happening?

Regrettably, he broke away, and murmured in a low, raspy voice that stole every coherent thought from her mind, "Before I forget, I have something for you."

He reached for the jacket he'd hung by the back door and rummaged through the interior pocket, before producing the tin of love letters.

"You finished translating them?" Her heart gave a tiny shudder of anticipation. She'd nearly forgotten all about them.

"I did, but I have to warn you. They don't make for cheery reading."

"Really?" Her excitement dwindled. For some reason, she'd hoped for an epic love story.

"I'll let you read them for yourself, but I didn't want you to expect a happy ending and wind up disappointed."

"Thanks. I appreciate that." She set the tin of letters on the counter behind her, suddenly not as interested in the outcome as when she'd first discovered them.

Sliding her arms around Landon's shoulders, she picked up where they'd left off. She was finally living her own love story, and she had a feeling it would have the happiest ending of them all.

When Landon returned home later that night, he barely remembered how he got there. He'd spent the entire drive reliving his evening with Sadie. He'd had some incredible experiences in his lifetime, from sailing a yacht around the world to spending ninety minutes in space, but nothing compared to being with Sadie. He didn't care what the activity entailed. Although he'd recently planned an adventure he couldn't wait to reveal, and hoped to surprise Sadie at the Sips & Sweets Festival.

Whistling to himself, he skipped up the porch steps, surprised to find Reggie barking at the front door.

"What is it, buddy?" He crouched to scratch behind his ear, but Reggie barked all the more frantically.

A sinking feeling settled in the pit of his stomach.

"Gladys?" he called out before remembering she had the night off.

His heart pounding, Landon stood, and the agitated pup nipped at his pant leg, tugging toward the hallway.

Trying to remain calm, he headed for the library, but halfway there, he broke into a run. Bursting into the room, he zeroed in on his mother's favorite spot by the fireplace. He froze, icy fear replacing all the blood in his veins.

His mother lay slumped in her wheelchair, her eyes closed, body limp.

He cried out as he rushed to her side, but she didn't respond.

Fighting the overwhelming panic rising in his chest, he called her name again as he checked her pulse, his palms slick with sweat.

Still no response, but he found a faint heartbeat. And she was still breathing.

He tried to steady his own breath, which came in quick, ragged spurts.

"I'm getting you to the hospital," he told her, though he didn't know if she could hear him.

But talking kept him calm.

With the afghan wrapped around her waist, he hoisted her into his arms, knocking something from her lap.

A familiar heart-shaped chocolate box fell to the floor, scattering empty wrappers like shrapnel.

A cold dread slithered through him, but he didn't have time to dwell on the implications.

With swift, fear-fueled strides, he headed for the door.

He could only pray it wasn't too late.

CHAPTER 24

Sadie set her mug of Earl Grey on the side table before nestling into the corner of the couch. The fire crackled in the hearth, dispelling the early morning chill, and Truffle and BonBon snoozed on the cushion beside her, creating a cozy atmosphere to finally read the long-anticipated letters. But even as she opened the tin, she knew she'd find it too difficult to concentrate. Her thoughts kept drifting to last night. She could still taste Landon's lips on hers. Not to mention the most delectable hot chocolate known to mankind.

She smiled to herself, envisioning the looks on the judges' faces when they took their first sip. While she didn't want to jinx her chances, she had a pretty good feeling she'd take home the grand prize, which would be one problem solved. The other issue yet to be resolved was Landon's shop next door. She still wasn't sure how they'd manage a budding relationship and the tension of rival businesses, but she finally had hope for the impossible.

Realizing she'd let her mind wander again, she plucked a

letter from the top of the stack and unfolded it on her lap. She only had a few hours before she needed to prepare for the festival and wanted to finish as many of them as she could.

But no sooner than she'd read *Dear Lise,* there was a knock at the door.

"Good morning!" She greeted Lucy with a smile, but it faded when she saw the somber look on her friend's face. "What's wrong?"

"There's something I need to tell you." Lucy slipped inside, not bothering with a formal hello. "Can we sit down?"

"Of course." A chill of apprehension swept over her. "Can I get you something to drink?"

Lucy shook her head, dropping onto the couch without removing her coat or hat. "I had an appointment at Mountain Crest Hospital this morning."

"Oh." Sadie collapsed onto the edge of the cushion, her knees suddenly too weak to support her. A familiar tightness constricted her throat. The kind that meant tears would soon follow.

"I'm okay," Lucy said hastily, reacting to Sadie's look of dismay. "It's not about me. It's..." She hesitated, then added softly, "It's Irene."

For a moment, Sadie couldn't move, as if a heavy weight had wrapped around her, slowly compressing her chest until she could no longer breathe.

"Sadie?" Lucy placed a hand on her shoulder, her voice laced with concern. "Are you okay?"

"What happened?" Sadie whispered, already imagining every worst-case scenario.

"I don't know. I ran into Landon in the hallway, but he didn't have much information. He..." She trailed off again, as though searching for a gentler way to deliver the news.

Except, there wasn't one. "He found her unconscious when he returned home last night. The doctors are running tests."

Sadie squeezed her eyes shut, wishing she could materialize a reset button, desperate to escape back in time when everyone was safe and happy.

"I'm so sorry, Sadie. I know how much she means to you. Want me to go to the hospital with you?"

The hospital....

She had a vision of Irene lying pale and lifeless in a stark, shapeless gown, and she suddenly felt ill. "I can't," she murmured, her voice breaking.

"Can't what?"

"I can't go to the hospital."

"I understand," Lucy said gently, rubbing her back. "You need time. We can wait a bit and then—"

"No, you don't understand." The words erupted in a strangled sob. "I can't go. Not today. Not ever. I can't do it, Luce. What if I lose her? I'm not strong enough to go through this again." Hot tears spilled down her cheeks, scorching her skin.

Irene had just gotten her life back, how could this be happening?

She clutched her heart, willing the pain to stop, but it merely ached all the more. Although Gigi had raised her and loved her dearly, their dynamic had always been one of a grandmother and granddaughter. But with Irene, she'd experienced a tiny taste of having a mother again, and she couldn't bear to lose her, too.

"I understand more than you think," Lucy murmured, and something in her inflection—a raw vulnerability—drew Sadie's gaze to her face. "When I first met with the doctor about my migraines, he warned me the cause might be something serious. I tried to be optimistic, choosing to believe I'd be okay. But there were a few times I let my fear take over. And in those dark moments, I wanted to hide from everyone I loved because I couldn't handle the thought of saying goodbye for good."

A sinewy streak of wet mascara marred Lucy's usually flawless features, and Sadie reached for her hand, giving it a comforting squeeze. "I had no idea you felt that way."

Lucy shrugged, blotting her damp cheek with the edge of her scarf. "Those feelings didn't last long, although they were devastating in the moment. Which is why I can honestly say I understand the temptation to push people away, hoping to protect yourself from even more pain. But the truth is, we need each other. I realized I would never regret the time I spent with my loved ones. Only the time I squandered."

Sadie sat in silence, mulling over Lucy's revelation.

Deep down, her words rang true.

But was she strong enough to accept them?

Standing in the hallway of the hospital, Landon listened to the doctor, both hands stuffed inside his pockets, his muscles tense.

"Your mother has a condition called diabetic ketoacidosis. In this state, her body doesn't have enough insulin to use the sugar in her blood. Instead, it breaks down fat for energy. This produces chemicals called ketones, which makes her blood more acidic. We've given her fluid and electrolytes, and with the addition of insulin therapy, she should be able to go home in one to three days."

"Thank you, Doctor." He glanced through the smudged glass separating them from his mother's hospital room.

Although stable, she drifted in and out of sleep. The sight of her pale features and plethora of tubes and wires attached to her frail body filled him with an overwhelming mixture of fear, guilt, and anger—anger he couldn't explain or fully understand, which only served to make him feel even more helpless.

"Moving forward, it's imperative that your mother takes her insulin and is mindful of her diet. Do you understand?"

"Yes, sir." His fist coiled around the ribbon in his pocket. The ribbon he'd found tangled in his mother's afghan. The telltale red ribbon with gold filigree.

When their conversation concluded, he watched the doctor retreat down the hallway, rounding the corner as another figure appeared.

Sadie rushed toward him, her face etched with worry. "How is she? Is she all right? I'm so sorry, Landon."

Her arms encircled him, and for a brief moment, he wanted to surrender to her touch, to release all the tension and anguish simmering beneath the surface. But he couldn't. He loved Sadie more than he'd ever thought possible, but he'd been foolish to think they could be together.

When his father left, he'd made a promise to himself. To protect his mother at all costs. Sadie would never give up chocolate. And he could never ask her to. But sugar and his mother were mutually exclusive. He'd allowed the two worlds to merge and look at what happened.

When he didn't return her embrace, Sadie stepped back, her gaze questioning. "Are you okay?"

Her soft, tentative tone hinted at the undercurrent of her question—the deeper meaning.

Was he okay? Were *they* okay?

He wasn't sure how to answer her, and when he finally

summoned a response, his words were brisk and perfunctory. "The doctors think she'll be fine, but she needs to take better care of herself."

"Can I see her?"

"I don't think that's a good idea." His inflection sounded colder than he'd intended.

"Of course. She needs rest." She hesitated a moment before asking, "Tomorrow, then?"

The ribbon burned like a hot coal in his pocket, branding his palm. He should walk away. He should excuse himself before he said something he'd regret. Exhausted and emotionally weary, he had no business having any conversations right now, let alone such a life-altering one.

"Landon?" Sadie searched his face, concern and confusion flickering in her gaze.

"I don't think you should see my mother for a while."

She flinched, unable to hide her shock. "Why?"

He scrunched his eyes shut as if he could block out the pain, but it clawed through his chest, wrenching his heart in two.

Forcing his eyes open, he withdrew the ribbon from his pocket and placed it in her hand.

Sadie stared at the clump of red and gold cradled in her palm, her features crumbling as she pieced together the implication.

Remorse slammed against his rib cage.

What had he just done?

CHAPTER 25

Cradling his head in both hands, Landon slumped in the creaky, uncomfortable chair, mired in his regrets.

The throbbing of his temples kept tune with the steady beeping of the heart monitor. He still couldn't believe he'd walked away from Sadie, shutting the door behind him. Shutting the door on his future. On everything he wanted most.

I want my mother to be healthy, he reminded himself, lifting his head to study her profile in the harsh light of the hospital room.

She stirred beneath the stiff sheets, her eyelids fluttering open.

He shot upright, reaching for her hand. "How are you feeling?"

"Exhausted. How long have I been asleep?"

"Most of the day."

"How's Reginald?"

"Being spoiled rotten by Gladys."

She smiled at the news, but it quickly faded. "Why aren't you at the festival?"

"Because I want to be here with you." How could she even ask him that?

"What about Sadie? Aren't you helping her with the contest?"

A pang of guilt stabbed his chest, followed by sharp, bitter disappointment. He'd been looking forward to today. Not only had he planned to help Sadie win the competition, but he had more than one surprise in store for her. Now, they were all meaningless. "We set up most of the booth and perfected the recipe yesterday. She'll be fine without me." *When it comes to the festival and the future,* he silently added.

As if reading his mind, she regarded him closely. "Did something happen between you two?"

"I'd rather not talk about it. Especially right now." He busied himself by pouring her a glass of water from the plastic pitcher. "Here. Drink this." He passed her the tiny paper cup, but she wasn't buying his deflection.

"What did you do?" She shot him a pointed stare, and he sighed, realizing he'd never escape her persistence.

"Mom, I know about the chocolates."

"I figured as much," she said with a look of quiet resignation. "But you need to know, they had nothing to do with Sadie. They were a gift from Bill."

"Bill?" His jaw clenched.

Irene set the cup on the side table without taking a sip. "Before you get angry with him, too, he doesn't know about my diabetes yet. I figured I'd save that for our third date." She offered a wry smile, adding, "For all he knew, the chocolates were a sweet and romantic gesture."

"Because greedy corporations have brainwashed people into believing flowers and chocolates are the only way to express affection." He sprang from the chair, both fists clenched at his sides as he paced the floor. Why hadn't he seen a situation like this coming? He should have been more aware and done something to prevent it. Instead, he'd been too caught up in his own life to look out for his mother the way he should have, the way he'd promised.

"Sweetheart, sit down." The grief in his mother's tone caught him by surprise.

"Are you okay?" He perched on the edge of the chair, leaning forward to take her hand again.

"No, I'm not." Tears welled in her eyes, and Landon's pulse raced.

"Mom, what's wrong? Do I need to call the nurse?"

"No, this is between me and you. A mother and her son." Her voice crackled with emotion. "I'm afraid I haven't been a very good mother lately."

"What are you talking about? You're the best." He gently squeezed her clammy fingers as apprehension slithered through him. Where had all this sadness and self-deprecation come from?

She shook her head, sniffling as she struggled to contain her tears. "Ever since your father left, you've taken it upon yourself to be my knight in shining armor, putting my needs above your own. And selfishly, I've let you."

"Mom—"

"No, sweetheart. Let me finish." Landon obeyed but kept a tight grip on her hand. "For most of my life, I've had an unhealthy relationship with food, particularly sweets. I've always known it about myself but pretended otherwise. Your father begged me to get help, but his insistence only made me dig my heels in deeper, and it tore our family apart."

A familiar fury surged in Landon's chest, and he couldn't

remain silent a second longer. "It's not your fault Dad left," he growled. The fingers of his free hand dug into his palm, leaving a mark.

"I know it's not. That's not what I'm saying." She looked toward the ceiling, teardrops collecting on her lashes. When she lowered her gaze, the sorrowful glint in her eyes gutted him to his core. "I'm not responsible for your father's actions. But I am responsible for my own. Or, more accurately, my *in*action. I've ignored my issues for too long, at the expense of the people I love most. You've been angry at the world, Landon. When the person you should be angry with... is me."

Landon gaped at her, unable to believe what he was hearing. And yet, his heart didn't balk as much as he'd expected. Could there be a grain of truth in her words?

He struggled to swallow past the tightness of his throat. "I've only ever wanted you to be healthy because I kinda like having you around."

"I know," she said softly. "You've made my health a priority, and it's time I do the same."

As she spoke, a floodgate opened, drenching him in a wave of rejuvenating relief he didn't know he needed. For so long, he'd buried his emotions, denying the twinge of pain and rejection each time she ignored the doctor's advice, each time she acted like she didn't care whether she lived or died. "You mean it?"

"I do." She smiled through her tears. "I want you to schedule an appointment with the therapist you've been hounding me about."

Her voice carried a teasing quality, and he would have laughed if he wasn't on the verge of crying himself. "You got it."

"But first." She shot him a meaningful glance. "Isn't there somewhere else you need to be?"

Knowing exactly what she meant, he stood. And with a full heart, he bent and gently kissed her forehead. "I love you, Mom."

"I love you, too. Now, go and get our girl."

As he strode out of the room, he prayed he still had a chance.

~

Returning from the hospital, Sadie silently slipped through the front door and tiptoed up the staircase, not wanting to alert Gigi to her presence.

She couldn't bear to discuss what happened between her and Landon. She wanted to pretend it was all a bad dream.

Deep down, she knew he'd reacted out of pain and concern for his mother. He'd built his entire life around caring for her, and in some ways, she found his actions admirable. But when he'd handed her that ribbon, implying she'd been complicit in what happened to Irene…

At the thought, a sob rose in her throat, and the second the door latched behind her, she freed her pent-up emotions, weeping so hard her shoulders shook.

Crumpling onto the bed, she curled into her pillow, burying her face in the soft cotton folds. When she finally cried her last tear, she sat upright, brushing aside the wisps of hair that clung to her damp cheek. She needed to pull herself together if she wanted to make it to the festival on time. And considering it was her only hope of saving the sweet shop, she couldn't afford to be late. Yet, her limbs wouldn't budge.

Her gaze fell on the tin of letters resting on her nightstand where she'd returned them for safekeeping earlier that morning. The anguish of Abélard's first letter flooded her mind. For once in her life, she knew exactly how he felt. And their mournful comradery compelled her to pry open the lid.

She carefully lifted the bundle of originals, setting them aside on the duvet. The neatly folded stack of Landon's translations stared up at her, taunting her with his crisp, even handwriting—the handwriting of a successful, assured businessman who knew exactly what he wanted. And he didn't want her.

With a macabre fascination, she pored over each letter, her heart commiserating with every wounded word. As much as she longed to go back in time, returning to her previous state of bliss, she knew it wasn't possible. Like Abélard, she had to face reality. She and Landon would never be, not anymore.

There was too much to forgive. Too much to overcome.

When she opened the last letter, her dry eyes couldn't shed another tear. Her raw, swollen throat could hardly swallow. Her heart felt numb.

Every ounce of hope had slipped from her grasp.

Just as it had for Abélard.

With an aching sense of finality, she read his heart-wrenching farewell.

After all this time, I suppose I must face the truth. You're not coming back to me.

You always say hot chocolate is for love that is lost. But there isn't enough hot chocolate in the world to mend this broken heart.

Goodbye, my love.

Know I'll always be yours.
Faithfully,
Your Abélard

Stunned, Sadie's gaze flew back a few lines.

Hot chocolate is for love that is lost.

Her grandmother's saying!

It wasn't a common colloquialism. How on earth had this man quoted the same expression? Had they been friends during her time in France?

Or…

At the knock on the door, Sadie jumped.

Gigi poked her head inside. "What are you still doing home? Shouldn't you be—" Her words fell away at the sight of Sadie's tear-stained face. "What's wrong, chérie?"

Sadie gestured to the letters. "Why didn't you tell me these were yours?"

For a long, painfully silent moment, Gigi didn't answer. Then, with a heavy sigh, her slender body slumped onto the edge of Sadie's bed. Gingerly, she lifted one of the letters, pinching the edges between her fingertips as though handling a delicate butterfly wing. "I never wanted you to find these."

"Why not? Who is Lise?"

"I am," Gigi murmured, her glassy eyes traveling over the worn pages.

"You?" Sadie breathed, sure she'd misheard.

"It's a pet name from the film *An American in Paris*. Although, I always told Abélard it didn't make sense since Lise is a Frenchwoman and Gene Kelly's character is the American." She gave a small shake of her head, her smile distant as she revisited her memories.

"But if you're Lise..." Sadie paused, trying to fit the pieces together. "Then that makes Abélard—"

"*Mon amour.* The love of my life. His father owned the chocolaterie where I studied in Paris. We fell in love instantly. First, over chocolate. But it became so much more."

Shocked, Sadie sank against the pillows. Her whole life, she'd believed Gigi had been above sentiments like love and romance. The kind of woman who'd thrived on her own, bucking tradition and societal expectations. She'd never once mentioned falling in love, let alone so deeply. "I had no idea. Why keep it from me? Why hide the letters in the wall?"

"I couldn't bear to destroy them." Gigi closed her eyes, inhaling the faint scent of cologne that lingered on the thick stationery. Regretfully, she placed the letters back inside the tin, replacing the lid. "But I couldn't risk you discovering them in the house. So, one day, when I had some work done in the kitchen, I sensed an opportunity. I hid them inside the wall, sure you'd never find them."

"But I still don't understand. Why keep them a secret? Why didn't you want me to know about you and Abélard?" If she'd known, would she have lived her life any differently?

Gigi contemplated her answer, choosing her words carefully. "Because I never wanted you to wonder if I regretted my decision."

What did she mean by her decision?

Sadie glanced from the tin back to Gigi, comprehension crashing into her with an unforgiving force. Abélard's fervent beseeching... the unrelenting heartbreak... the love lost... all of it... was because of *her*.

Fresh tears sprang to her eyes, and Gigi grasped her hand, her own eyes glistening. "This is why I wanted the letters to remain a secret. I never wanted you to question your place in this world. Or my heart. If I could go back in time, I'd leave Paris again. A thousand times. Because raising you has been the greatest blessing of my life. I'm so proud to be your grandmother, first and foremost. Never, ever doubt that."

As Gigi spoke, Sadie's tears fell hard and fast, but she didn't bother wiping them away. She'd always known Gigi had made sacrifices to raise her after her parents died. And she'd tried to be worthy of those sacrifices. But her grandmother had given up so much more than she'd realized. And how had she repaid her? By losing the legacy she'd worked so hard to build.

Overcome with shame and remorse, she whispered, "You shouldn't be proud. I don't deserve it." She dragged her fingers across her cheeks, roughly smudging her tears.

"Why on earth would you say such a thing?" Gigi sounded horrified.

"I'm in debt at the sweet shop." Her hoarse confession burned her throat. "I had to replace some expensive equipment and things sort of snowballed out of my control. If I win the contest today, I can pay some of it back. But it's not a guarantee."

"Oh, chérie. Why didn't you tell me? I can help."

"That's exactly why I didn't say anything. You've done so much for me already. If I told you, you'd use your travel funds to pay off the debts. And I couldn't let you do that. It's my responsibility. You left your legacy in my hands, and I didn't want to let you down. But now, it looks like I have." Just as she dried her eyes, more tears tumbled down her cheeks.

"My darling girl," Gigi said softly, cupping Sadie's chin with her fingertips. "The sweet shop isn't my legacy. *You* are." Speechless, Sadie met her gaze, and Gigi's smile deepened. "I couldn't be prouder of the woman you've become. You're kind, courageous, hardworking, and considerate. You're full of life and love toward others. And I plan on taking some of the credit for how well you turned out."

She winked, and to Sadie's surprise, a ripple of light, cleansing laughter bubbled to the surface, rinsing away a burden she'd carried for years. All this time, she'd tried to earn back the price her grandmother had paid, to be worthy of her sacrifices by following in her footsteps. And yet, her grandmother had given her love freely. Joyfully. The guilt had been a burden of her own making. "Are you really not upset about the shop?"

"I'm more upset you didn't feel you could come to me."

"You're right. I'm so sorry I didn't tell you."

"And I'm sorry I wasn't more forthcoming about my past."

Sadie kneaded her bottom lip, hoping for one last ounce of clarity. Exhaling a deep breath, she said, "Please don't be mad, but I have to ask. After reading Abélard's letters, and seeing how deeply he cared about you, do you really not have any regrets?"

"I'll never regret leaving Paris to raise you. But I do sometimes wonder if I gave up on love too easily. At the time, our situation seemed hopeless. You needed to be here, with your friends and your school. And Abélard needed to take over the chocolaterie that had been in his family for five generations. But perhaps, if I'd written him back..." She trailed off with a faraway look, then shrugged, snapping herself back to the present. "Oh, well. What's done is done. I don't believe in dwelling on the past." She paused, then added, "But I do believe this. If you're fortunate enough to find the kind of love that enriches your life and makes you better than you were before… Well, that is a love worth fighting for. With everything you have."

She patted Sadie's cheek, adding, "Now, ma chérie, don't you have somewhere you need to be?"

CHAPTER 26

Landon scanned the crowded town square, searching for Sadie.

Canopy-covered booths representing artisanal sweets from Poppy Creek and the surrounding towns lined all four streets. Landon spotted everything from honeysuckle wine infused with real gold flecks to pink lemonade pie with candied poppy petals.

But no sign of Sadie.

He wove past a taffy pulling demonstration and a vendor sampling rosemary citrus sorbet as he headed to their assigned spot on the far corner of Main Street. When his gaze landed on the unfinished display, his heart sank.

Where was Sadie?

She wouldn't miss the competition, but the judges had already started reviewing the entries.

At the table next to theirs, Eliza arranged generous slices of lavender honey cheesecake drizzled with a strawberry balsamic sauce. Beside her, Cassie prepared the ingredients for her cardamom rose latte. She appeared to be dying the milk pink with beetroot powder. Their entire booth resembled a lush garden in the dead of winter, and he had to hand it to the ladies. They'd be strong competition. Although, he still felt Sadie's hot chocolate and the elaborate Parisian theme they'd planned for their presentation would blow them out of the water.

So, where was she?

"Have you seen Sadie?" he asked, forgoing a greeting. With the judges only a few booths behind, he didn't have time for chitchat.

Cassie glanced up in surprise. "She's on her way to the hospital to see you."

"What? Are you sure?"

"Positive. She called a few minutes ago to let us know."

Eliza set down her serving knife and joined the conversation. "She asked us to apologize to Mayor Burns for her, knowing he'd be upset that there was no one at your booth. She was positive you'd still be at the hospital with your mom."

Was there a slight accusatory edge to her voice? Landon wasn't sure. He could hardly focus on anything except for the knowledge that Sadie had forfeited the competition… for him.

A tingling warmth spread across his body.

He still had a chance to make things right.

His gaze darted down the row of competitors. Mayor Burns led his cohorts of fellow judges in a tasting of what looked like some kind of baked Alaska flambé. "How much time do you think we have until the judges get here?"

"Not long," Cassie estimated. "Why? Do you still plan on entering?"

"Not exactly. I have something else in mind." He pushed up his sleeves. "But I might need some help."

Without hesitation, Cassie wiped both hands on her apron and asked, "What can we do?"

~

Riddled with nerves, Sadie paused in the hallway to collect herself.

What if Landon told her to leave again? What if he wouldn't listen to what she had to say?

What *did* she have to say?

Every line she'd rehearsed on the drive to Primrose Valley suddenly evaporated into thin air, leaving her with only one thought.

I love you. And I believe you love me. Whatever issues we have, we can work through them. Together.

Inhaling sharply, she squared her shoulders and strode toward Irene's room, willing her body to put one foot in front of the other, despite her unease.

She pushed through the door, her heartbeat stammering, to find Irene alone. Her surprise immediately gave way to a wave of other emotions at seeing her reclined in the hospital bed surrounded by ominous medical equipment.

She swallowed against the sudden catch in her throat.

Hearing her enter, Irene stirred, smiling when she spotted her in the doorway. "Sadie. What a nice surprise."

"How are you?" Tentative, she crept forward. Irene looked tired, but her cheeks had some color, which Sadie took as a positive sign.

"I'm fine, dear. Don't look so worried. The real question is, what are you doing here? Aren't you supposed to be at the festival?"

Sadie unraveled her scarf, settling on the chair by Irene's

bedside. "I'd rather be here. I'm so sorry about what happened."

"Don't be silly. You have nothing to be sorry about. I only have myself to blame. Besides," she added, "this experience has given me the final push I needed to take better care of myself. And if I can stick with a healthy routine, I promised Landon I'd look into the possibility of a pancreas transplant."

"Oh, Irene, that would be wonderful! I'm sure you can do it. And I'll help any way I can." Sadie beamed, knowing Landon would be beyond thrilled. "Speaking of Landon, is he here?" She glanced at the clock. It was nearing lunchtime already. Maybe he was grabbing a quick bite at the cafeteria?

"Actually, he left a little while ago. To see you, in fact."

"He did?"

"It may not be my place to say," Irene said in a tone indicating she had zero qualms about butting in, "but Landon feels terrible about what happened between you two. Goodness knows, he isn't perfect. But he never meant to hurt you."

"I know," Sadie said softly. Had Landon really left his mother's bedside to see her? His absence spoke volumes, filling her heart with a warm fuzziness.

"Did you also know he's madly in love with you?"

Sadie nearly fell off her chair. What had Irene said?

"Way to steal my thunder, Mom."

Sadie froze at the sound of Landon's voice. Her heart stuttering, she slowly swiveled to face him.

He stood in the doorway, holding something small and shiny in his hands. But she couldn't focus. She couldn't breathe. He looked at her with such tender intensity, every nerve in her body shut down, leaving her immobile.

Without taking his eyes off her, he spanned the distance

between them, stopping mere inches away. "Although she spoke out of turn, my mother wasn't wrong. Sadie Hamilton, you're the most captivating, infuriating, incredible, unparalleled woman I've ever met. And I've been the biggest fool on the planet. I don't deserve your forgiveness, but I'm going to ask for it, anyway. Because in the last several weeks, you've turned my life upside down. And the truth is, I like it better this way." His voice grew deeper, husky with emotion as he added, "I love you, Sadie. And if you'll let me, I'll spend the rest of my days showing you exactly how much. Even if it means eating chocolate." The most endearing, lopsided smile accompanied his last words, and every ounce of hesitation and doubt melted away.

Before her mind could form a response, she found herself in his arms, surrendering to his kiss. Passionate yet soft and sweet, his lips teased hers, increasing in earnestness as his fingertips traced the nape of her neck, scattering goose bumps across her skin. For a moment, she forgot where she was, wholly engrossed in the feel of his body, his kiss, the intoxicating scent of him.

Irene cleared her throat, breaking the spell, and Sadie broke away, flushed and blissfully breathless. But Landon refused to let her go. Pressing his forehead to hers, he waited a beat before pulling back, his dark eyes muddied with longing.

"I'd offer to give you two some privacy, but this bed isn't as easy to maneuver as my wheelchair," Irene teased.

Sadie blushed and took a step back, smoothing her rumpled hair.

Landon straightened, and for the first time, she registered the polished trophy in his hand.

The *first-place* trophy.

"You won the Tastiest Treat competition?" She couldn't hide her surprise.

Landon grinned. "Actually, *you* did."

"How is that possible?"

"Cassie and Eliza put the finishing touches on the booth while I made the hot chocolate and entered it on your behalf. The judges had never seen—or tasted—anything like it. I have a feeling you won in a landslide vote."

She gazed up at him in disbelief. "You forfeited the competition for me?"

"No, you won fair and square. We just wanted you to have the opportunity you deserved."

Baffled and moved beyond words, she continued to gape at him, her mind whirling. "What about your grand opening? Wasn't that supposed to be today?"

"I decided to postpone. Indefinitely."

Her heart gave a strange little leap, not daring to hope. "How come?"

"I've decided to take it in a different direction." Setting the trophy aside, he took both of her hands in his. "Sadie, I have an important proposition to make. Instead of opening my own place, I'd like to invest in yours. What do you think about expanding Sadie's Sweet Shop?"

"What?" she gasped, barely able to breathe.

"I'd like to tear down the wall between us. Again. Only this time, I'd like it to be permanent. What do you say, Sade?"

She stared at their entwined fingers, acutely aware of the warmth and pressure of his palms against hers. His touch felt so strong, so secure. And he wasn't simply offering to save her shop—he was offering to fulfill her lifelong dream.

"Yes," she murmured, fighting happy tears, "under one condition."

"Name it."

"I want to add a line of healthier options. Not just sugar free, but for customers with allergies and food sensitivities, too. And I think we should have a few specialty items with a molecular gastronomy flair. Know anyone who could help with that?"

"I think I could find someone." His deep, playful tone sent pleasant shivers down her spine. "There's something else I'd like to add, as long as we're negotiating."

"I'll take it under consideration," she teased.

"With the new renovations, you'll have to close the shop for a few weeks. I propose we take a trip somewhere during the downtime. You, too, Mom." Landon tossed her a grin. "If you can bear to leave Reggie for that long."

"I appreciate the offer, sweetheart. But I think I'd rather stay home this time." Irene blushed, and Sadie didn't have to guess why. A certain tall, soft-spoken farmer sprang to mind.

"Are you thinking of somewhere specific?" she asked Landon, her heart fluttering at the thought of exploring the world together.

"Very specific." He reached into his coat pocket and withdrew a small envelope, handing it to her with an excited energy.

Her pulse thrummed in anticipation as she slid out the tiny note card.

Stunned, she read the name and address several times, unable to believe her eyes. "You found Abélard?"

"Yep. I'd asked a friend to look after you mentioned how neat it would be to track him down to see if he wanted the letters back. It's surprising the kind of information you can find online, if you know how to look. He's in his late eighties, never been married, and guess what? He owns a chocolate shop. I thought, why not take a trip and meet him in person?"

"I can't believe you did this for me." She stared at the Paris address, her mind reeling with an outlandish—and utterly exhilarating—idea. "Landon, would you mind if I invited Gigi to go with us?"

"Not at all. It would be nice to have someone who's more fluent in French than I am. Especially to speak with Abélard."

Oh, if only he knew! Smiling to herself, she tucked the note card back inside the envelope. She'd tell him about Gigi and Abélard later. For now, she wanted to bask in the indescribable magic of the moment.

"Thank you," she whispered, memorizing the tender glint in his eyes as he cupped her face, lowering his lips to hers.

Brimming with love and happiness, she melted into his kiss, her heart full of hope for the future.

EPILOGUE

With an expert hand, Cassie Davis sprinkled tiny purple buds on the creamy froth before sliding the mug across the counter where it was eagerly claimed by Grant. He'd already downed three of the lavender rose lattes, and she'd made this one decaf, knowing Eliza would thank her later.

"Thanks, Cass. These are addictive." He sipped the sweet concoction, which left behind a faint filmy mustache.

Cassie smiled as he rejoined the cluster of friends gathered around Reed and Olivia, who basked in the glow of their engagement party. Olivia, the consummate event coordinator, had already planned most of the wedding and cheerfully regaled them with the details. Filled with contentment, Cassie swept her gaze around the café, cherishing the sight of all her favorite people in one place.

Well, almost all of them.

Over the last few years, she'd slowly mended fences with her mother, who'd finally turned a corner in her battle with alcoholism. While some wounds still needed time to heal, she'd witnessed genuine growth. And for the first time in her life, she'd experienced a loving mother-daughter relationship.

Except the elusive and enigmatic Donna Hayward refused to step foot in Poppy Creek for more than a day or two at a time. And during each brief and infrequent visit, an air of apprehension had hovered around her like an ominous cloud threatening a dangerous hailstorm. But the most frustrating part? Her mother never explained why, no matter how tirelessly Cassie asked.

But then again, Donna had a habit of keeping secrets.

For as long as Cassie could remember, she'd begged for information about her father. His name, occupation, whether he preferred mayonnaise or mustard—anything. As far as she knew, she'd never even met the man—not once. Not even as a baby. He'd simply vanished from their lives, almost as if he'd never existed. And all her attempts to find him had turned up empty.

Topping another latte with edible lavender buds, Cassie carried it toward the cozy group by the front window. Raindrops beaded against the glass, shimmering in the soft, ambient light, and for a moment, Cassie paused, savoring the charming vignette. Three couples, all rapturous smiles and loving gazes, chatted among themselves, encapsulated in a bubble of pure bliss.

"I still can't believe it," Irene gushed. "You two are a living, breathing romance novel."

Bill stood by her side, one hand gently resting on her shoulder as they stared at Gigi and her dashing date in delighted amazement. Gigi's youthful blush took ten years off her face, and the age-defying woman already looked decades younger than her counterparts.

Cassie would be the first to admit the two lovebirds made an adorable couple. The wiry-framed Frenchman, with his silver hair and neatly trimmed beard, had an effortless, sleek style that complemented Gigi's more flamboyant fashion sense. She had a feeling they'd turned heads in their younger years, gallivanting through the cobblestone streets of Paris.

The man—who Gigi had introduced as Abélard Dupont—said something in French, which made Gigi's blush deepen. At their curious expressions, he repeated himself in broken English. "Not even the greatest poet could capture our love story. It would not be believed."

"What did you think the very first moment you saw Gigi enter your chocolate shop?" Cassie joined their conversation as she handed the latte to Sadie.

Her friend accepted it with a smile, remaining tucked beneath Landon's arm, where she'd spent most of the night. In fact, Cassie couldn't recall a time they'd been apart all evening. The realization made her heart swell with happiness.

"I thought nothing, at first," he admitted. "I often saw her in my dreams, waking or sleeping, made no difference."

Cassie nearly melted at the romantic sentiment. Frenchmen really did know how to make a girl swoon.

"But when she spoke, I knew I now lived in my dream, never to wake up again."

"Does that mean you're staying in Poppy Creek?" she asked.

"For some time. And we will spend some time in Paris. And some time traveling the world."

"His godson runs the chocolaterie now," Gigi explained, gazing up at him with the most adoring expression.

"And to think," Irene interjected, her voice filled with wonderment, "all of this happened thanks to the software program Landon's friend invented. As much as I distrust technology that can find anyone at any time, I'm certainly grateful for the intrusion in this instance."

Cassie's pulse thrummed. "Can it really find anyone?"

"That's the claim," Landon said casually. "And it worked like a charm in this case, so I'm inclined to believe him."

Cassie let his words sink in, her heart racing.

Could it be possible?

And if it was, did she have the nerve to ask Landon for such a big favor?

She straightened, a sense of resolve forming in the pit of her stomach.

She would do it. She would ask Landon to find her father.

Donna Hayward rolled onto her back, relaxing into a final Savasana pose on her faded yoga mat. The roof of her San Francisco apartment complex towered above the nearby buildings, and without a shade barrier, the early morning sun bathed her face and neck.

Although wary of wrinkles—her skin in her late forties wasn't what it used to be—she welcomed the warmth. It made her feel alive, which she found slightly ironic considering she was in a supine yoga position that literally translated to *corpse pose*.

Sirens, car horns, and the rumble of a garbage truck invaded her senses, but she skillfully blocked out the noise, trying to clear her mind. Yoga had been invaluable during her detox from alcohol, and she continued the practice even in sobriety. Mind over matter became her philosophy.

But while she'd managed to wrangle her addiction into

daily, minute-by-minute, submission, she could never fully achieve a restful mental state. Whenever she tried, her regrets grew louder in the silence.

And she had a lot of regrets.

A timer beeped on her phone, and her eyes flew open.

"Thanks for another great session." Her friend Monica rose from her mat and swallowed a few gulps from her water bottle before gathering her belongings.

Donna met the ex-lawyer at an Alcoholics Anonymous meeting a few months ago. After a bender, she'd lost her job, and her parents took temporary custody of her kids until she "got her life under control."

When Donna mentioned how yoga helped with her sobriety, Monica expressed an interest but couldn't afford the rates at an official studio. Feeling for her plight, Donna offered personal coaching every morning before her waitressing shift, which then led to her teaching a regular class every weekend for other women in recovery.

"I get to see my kids today." Monica hooked the strap of her gym bag over her shoulder, grinning as she shared the news.

"That's wonderful." Donna smiled, genuinely happy for her friend. Although, she couldn't help a tiny pang of envy.

She rarely saw her daughter, who was fully grown now. And for the majority of her life, she'd been a terrible mother, so consumed by her own trauma, she blindly inflicted pain on the one person who needed her most.

No matter how desperately she longed to make amends and recapture some of what they'd lost, how could they truly reconnect when she couldn't be entirely honest?

Her secret would forever be a divide.

And yet, she'd take it to her grave.

If not for her sake…
Then for her daughter's.

YOU CAN CONTINUE THE STORY IN THE PROMISE IN POPPIES. VISIT rachaelbloome.com/the-promise-in-poppies FOR MORE INFORMATION.

ACKNOWLEDGMENTS

There were days I wondered if I'd ever finish this book. Between morning sickness and adjusting to life with a newborn, I wasn't sure I'd have the time, energy, or mental clarity to piece together a coherent story, let alone a novel worthy of publication.

Without the patient encouragement of my friends and family, you wouldn't be reading this today.

So, first and foremost, I'd like to thank my husband—you are my rock, my best friend, and my biggest supporter. Thank you for holding my hand all the way to the finish line.

To the best mom and mother-in-law a girl could ever ask for—thank you for all the hours you watched Violet so I could write. Although spending time with the sweetest, most beautiful baby in the world isn't exactly a chore, I appreciate you more than you'll ever know.

Dave Cenker—it continues to be an honor to be your critique partner. Not only did you offer invaluable feedback, but you freely gave your friendship and support. There were days when your notes alone gave me the motivation I needed to keep going. Thank you!

To my team—Ana, Krista, Beth, and Trenda—you went above and beyond, fitting me into your schedule at the last minute, since life was too hectic and uncertain to plan ahead. I will forever be grateful for your flexibility and generosity of time.

Violet—becoming your mother has completely changed my life and will forever impact how I see the world. And I know my writing will be richer because of you.

Lastly, dear reader—thank you for your patience and loyal support. This book has taken me SO much longer to publish than the others, but you've been so gracious as I've spent time with my daughter, putting our family first.

While life is one new adventure after another, and I have no idea what the future holds, I'm hopeful I'll be telling stories for many years to come.

And I hope you'll go on that journey with me.

If you enjoyed Sadie and Landon's story, **please consider leaving an honest review at the retailer of your choice**. It truly helps new readers find the series.

Until next time…

Blessings & Blooms,

Rachael Bloome

ABOUT THE AUTHOR

Rachael Bloome is a *hopeful* romantic. She loves every moment leading up to the first kiss, as well as each second after saying, "I do." Torn between her small-town roots and her passion for traveling the world, she weaves both into her stories—and her life!

Joyfully living in her very own love story, she enjoys spending time with her husband, daughter, and two rescue dogs, Finley and Monkey. When she's not writing, helping to run the family coffee roasting business, or getting together with friends, she's busy planning their next big adventure!

SADIE'S HOT CHOCOLATE RECIPE

Author note:

I've always loved hot chocolate.

While strolling the scenic streets of Paris on a crisp fall afternoon in 2018, Mr. Bloome and I stumbled upon an exquisite tea house called Angelina.

We each ordered the house hot chocolate to warm our frozen hands and inadvertently discovered the best hot chocolate of our lives.

While writing this story, I knew I wanted to pay homage to the not-so-little tea house I will forever hold fondly in my memory.

And although my recipe is not the same as the hot chocolate I savored in France, I hope it brings a little extra comfort on a cold day... or even a warm one!

RECIPE:

Makes 2 Servings

INGREDIENTS:

2 oz dark chocolate (either chips or a bar broken into small pieces)

2 oz white chocolate (same as dark chocolate)

1 cup 2% milk

1 cup heavy cream

1/4 cup brown sugar

1 tsp vanilla

1/2 tsp finely ground espresso

Instructions:

1. In a medium saucepan, combine milk, cream, sugar, and vanilla. Heat over medium heat until mixture steams and a thin film forms on the surface. Stir occasionally with wire whisk, approximately 4-5 minutes.

2. Add chocolate to the saucepan, whisking until chocolate has melted.

3. Reduce heat to medium-low. Add espresso and whisk continuously until mixture is frothy, approximately 3-4 minutes. Do not bring to a rolling boil.

4. Immediately remove from heat and pour into two mugs.

5. Allow to cool slightly before serving.

Enjoy!

Note:

This is a thick, decadent hot chocolate—dessert in a glass!

To *reduce* thickness, increase milk by 1/4 cup.

Or, if you really have a hankering for hot chocolate so thick, you'll need a spoon, substitute milk and cream with 2 cups of half-and-half.

Optional Garnishes:

Whipped cream

Caramel or fudge drizzle

Sprinkle of cinnamon or nutmeg

Marshmallows

For a CHILLED VERSION to enjoy in warmer months, allow hot chocolate to cool, then combine with crushed ice in a blender until it reaches a milkshake-like consistency.

BOOK CLUB QUESTIONS

1. What does hope mean to you?
2. Do you have a specific comfort food/drink?
3. Does a particular food evoke a special memory or person?
4. Do you believe opposites attract? Or is it more important for a couple to have similarities?
5. Which character did you find the most relatable?
6. If you had to fill out a card for the Saint Valentine Swap, what act of service would you offer?
7. If you found a box of secret letters, would you read them?
8. Have you ever made an enormous sacrifice for someone you love?
9. Have you ever felt the need to live up to someone else's ideal only to find out they were already proud of you?
10. What do you think is the theme of the book?

As always, I look forward to hearing your thoughts on the story. You can email your responses (or ask your own questions) at hello@rachaelbloome.com or post them in my private Facebook group, Rachael Bloome's Secret Garden Club.

Made in the USA
Coppell, TX
20 June 2022